In This Together

GOD OF THE VALLEYS AND MOUNTAINS

Cami Oller

In This Together: God of the Valleys and Mountains
Cover Design by: Cheryl Chaney
Editing by: Oller Publishing and Co.
Copyright © Carri Oller

This book is dedicated to my love. Matt, I love you so much. Thank you for being my best friend, adventure buddy, prayer partner, fishing partner, and for always being silly with me. You are my favorite. I adore you, my love. I love writing fictional characters that have a relationship like ours. I'm thankful to be your bride. I love growing old with you babe.

Yours forever,

Carri

In This Together

GOD OF THE VALLEYS AND MOUNTAINS

Carri Oller

Table of Contents

Chapter One

AARON

As the door opened, I felt a million emotions. I wanted to know what the doctor was going to say, and I was also terrified of what the doctor would say. But, when the doctor stepped into the room, I felt God's peace overflowing from the doctor. Even though I was terrified for my son, I knew in my heart that whatever was going to happen, God was in control. But there was a huge part of me that felt hopeless, like this entire situation was so out of control, and I didn't understand it.

I just wanted this not to be real...

Why did this have to happen?

Why did Blake and Jean have to die?

Why is my firstborn in this horrible and unthinkable situation?

Why can't I fix all of this?

God, why?

"Nick and Charlotte, my name is Dr. Miller, but you all can call me Chiquita. I first want you to know that we are doing everything we can for Aaron. Right now, we have him in a medically induced coma. He has some swelling on his brain, and we are trying to get that taken care of right now as we speak. He also has a couple of broken ribs and a broken tibia. He has coded one time, but right now, everything is as steady as it can be under the circumstances. We will keep him in a medically induced coma for a few days. Then we will slowly wake him up. I usually pray silently for my patients. Since I know, Charlotte is a pastor..."

Nick and I looked at each other, confused and wondering how she knew that. I think she could tell the confusion by our facial expressions.

"My husband and I visited your church last week. I'd love to pray with you both right now, if that's okay with you?" Chiquita asked.

I couldn't help but think, "Wow, even though this situation is heartbreaking and devastating, what an amazing thing to know that God connected us to Aaron's doctor before this even happened."

Nick and I were utterly devastated at this news. It almost felt as though we both had an out-of-body experience. I felt like I just got punched in the gut over and over. Could this really be happening? I felt like we were in a bad dream. I wanted so badly just to wake up in Nick's arms with him softly stroking my hair while telling me that it was just a bad dream.

But it wasn't a bad dream...
This was our reality...
This was really happening...
I felt so lost and confused...

Truthfully, I was battling with trusting God and feeling hopeless. We lost Blake and Jean. Were we going to lose Aaron too? It was all too much to bear.

Being the strong one, Nick said, "Yes, please, Chiquita, we would truly appreciate that."

I halfway smiled at Chiquita, trying to let her know that I appreciated her offering that comfort to us, and replied, "Yes, Chiquita, please do. I have no words right now. I don't even know how to pray right now."

Chiquita boldly said as she grabbed our hands, "Okay then. Let's do it. Lord, we come to you right now. We ask in the mighty name of Jesus that you will completely heal Aaron. Heal him, Lord, from the top of his head to the tips of his toes. No weapon formed against him will prosper in Jesus' name! God, we know that you are the God of the valleys and the mountains. I know Charlotte and Nick feel like they are in the deepest of valleys right now. But God, we know that regardless of the size of the obstacles, no obstacle is bigger than you, Lord. We believe that our faith in you, Lord, can move mountains on Aaron's behalf. Amen!"

Chiquita sweetly smiled, then gently said, "Remember you two, even when we don't know how or what to pray, God knows. He meets us where we are. Even our tears are prayers to God. He knows what we need. He knows it all. Even though we don't know exactly what is going to happen, we know that God is with each of us. Our faith is something that no situation and no person can take away from us. We will do anything and everything we can for your son, that is my promise to you all."

As I opened my eyes, I saw that all three of us had tears rolling down our cheeks. It's not too often that you see a doctor getting emotional like that. But I could tell that Aaron had a doctor that genuinely cared about her patients. That blessed my heart and gave me a glimpse of hope for our sweet boy.

Police officers do the same thing. They must try to be strong when talking to people and not show emotions. But there are times that emotions are seen. It's only human. I know that Nick has had several tough calls. There have been times where he has had to deliver the horrifc news that a family member passed away to families. I remember the horrific call he had a few months back. A three month old baby died. He was the first one to arrive on the scene. The mom of the baby didn't want to let her baby go. He held his emotions until he got in his patrol car, then he would call me and cry.

All first responders take on a lot in their time of

serving. We can all sometimes be overwhelmed with our feelings. I could tell that for Chiquita that this was one of those times. I think this tragic event will affect our community for a long time.

"Thank you Chiquita. We appreciate you." Nick responded.

"You two, let me know if I can do anything for you. In the meantime, please know we are doing everything in our power to help Aaron. Most of all, remember that our God is mighty. Remember that before Aaron was yours, he was God's. God has this. No matter what happens. God has this. Please feel free to invite your friends and family to come to this room. You all stay as long as you need," Chiquita said.

All I could do was give Chiquita a hug. I couldn't even come up with the words to speak. I appreciated her comforting prayer. I appreciated her compassion. I knew that Aaron was in good hands. I just hated this entire situation.

"Thank you again," Nick replied.

As Chiquita walked out of the room, Nick pulled me towards him. I buried my head in his chest and just started weeping. He kissed the top of my head and gently stroked my hair as he cried too. After a few minutes, I pulled my head up to look into Nick's eyes. We were both heartbroken. I could tell that Nick felt so helpless about it all. He wanted to save everyone.

He wanted to change it. But he couldn't, and neither could I.

"Babe, I think we should go ahead and text everyone that's here to come on in here. That way, we can brief them on what's going on." Nick said.

"Yeah, I think you're right babe. I'll text Roxy and have her spread the news to the everyone that's out there." I softly replied.

As I started texting Roxy, Nick started looking at his cell phone. He received several messages from the guys at the police division. They were all telling him about what the Chief did on behalf of our family.

"Wow! Look at this!" Nick said in an astonished voice.

Nick showed me his cell phone, "The Chief of Police just did a television interview with the local news station. He said in the interview that this event was one that hit close to home and told the story of what happened. He asked everyone for donations to help with hospital costs for Aaron. He also was asking for help from the community to help Blake's mother and Jean's family for funeral costs. They have collected over twenty-thousand dollars already."

"That is such a huge blessing. Wow, that means so much." I responded.

"I don't even know what to say to Blake's mom. I mean you would think that I would know what to say, but I really don't...not with this...not about Blake." Nick softly said.

It broke my heart to see him in such agony. He wanted so badly to fix everything and make it all better. Yet, he knew that he couldn't change it. He couldn't fix it. This was one of those seasons where we simply had to press into God more than ever before.

We heard a knock on the door. It gently opened. Before we knew what happened we had Roxy, Mark, Taylor, Zach, Violet, Will, Tommy, Julie, Jessica, Toby, Olivia, Jaron, Keith, Tracey, Anna, and Sean were all walking in the room to be with us.

When everyone walked in, they all hugged Nick and I and sat down in a chair. It felt as though we were all a bunch of sardines as we were all scrunched in this room together. Everyone's eyes were glued onto Nick and me.

Keith spoke first. He could tell that Nick and I were gathering our words to say. "Jordan is on his way here. Mark left his room to come down here. He told Dr. Stephens what was going on, so she gave him permission to leave his room. Erica and Tory are still being looked at with their injuries right now. But they are in good hands."

"Yeah, the doctor gave me permission, but I would have left anyway. I don't care," Mark replied in a goofy and snarky voice.

Everyone kind of giggled at Mark's goofy and confident deminer. He could always lighten the mood in the room with his morbid sense of humor.

Nick cleared his throat and said, "You all are a blessing to be here with us tonight. Tommy and Julie, we want you all to know that we are praying for Erica and Tory too. This has been a horrible event that will affect us forever. We lost Blake and Jean. Tory said that it looked like Jean sacrificed herself to try and save the kids. I know we will always be forever grateful for her sacrifice. If Blake and Aaron wouldn't have changed places...we..."

Nick began to weep...

Everyone was just sitting in silence. Many of them had tears going down their cheeks. Even though some of them knew exactly what happened, they knew Nick and I were trying to get everyone on the same page. So, everyone just sat reverent out of love and respect for us.

I touched Nick's arm, cleared my throat, and said, "Babe, I'll take it from here. We would have lost Aaron if the boys hadn't switched places. I don't know why the boys switched places. I know that Blake liked Tory, so he was probably trying to be silly, if I had to guess. Blake was always trying to make everyone laugh. When the car wreck happened, Jean apparently saw that Fred Duncan was coming toward them at a fast speed. She must have known he probably wasn't going to stop. So she pulled out, and Fred hit her car, which hit Aaron's car and then hit Tory's car...when...when..."

Nick, at this time, got his composure back and said, "It's okay...I got it from here, babe. When this happened, it killed Jean instantly; it caused Blake to hit his head extremely hard and have blunt force trauma to his head, which killed him instantly. It caused Aaron to have severe injuries, which we now have learned that he has swelling on his brain, along with a broken tibia and two broken ribs. Tory has severe hip pain and a concussion. Erica has a broken leg and a concussion. And somehow, Fred Duncan is just fine. With just a minor fracture of his wrist. Which I'm sorry, I think it's complete bullshit. How can Jean and Blake be killed, these kids be hurt, and this idiot be okay? I'm angry. I don't get it. So now Aaron is in a medically induced coma for a few days to see if they can relieve the swelling in his brain. I just want to hear Aaron's voice. I want to hug him. I want to play basketball with him. I just wish I could rewind time and make all of this not real, but I can't."

As everyone continued to listen, Keith and Tracey both got up. Tracey said, "There are no perfect words that we can give you all right now. But here's what we can give you. I know that everyone in this room loves you all and your family. You all are such an amazing couple and watching your faith during all this is going to not only witness to us, but to those around you. We are all hurting at this sudden loss of Jean and Blake. We are angry that they were killed because of someone's negligence. We are all hurting that Aaron, Erica, and Tory are hurting. I know it may feel like you all are alone in this, but I can assure you that you are not alone. First, we know God is with you all. Second, I know that everyone in this room, including all the Oklahoma City Police Department are all behind you all. Whatever you all need, we are here."

"Amen!" Roxy shouted.

"So, when exactly will they start trying to wake Aaron up?" Olivia asked.

"I'm guessing it will probably be Wednesday or Thursday," I replied.

"Okay, I will make sure to put him on the prayer list at church. Also, Charlotte don't worry about coming in for work this week. Just take this week off, honestly take as long as you need. We can cover the youth group," Tommy said.

Julie sweetly chimed in, "Absolutely. We will make sure everything is covered. Also, we would love to make your family meals this week. I know several volunteers at the church would also like to help get groceries for you all and help with the farm and animals this week. The Alexander's are excellent at assisting with all that stuff. I'm sure they would love to help. I'll contact them tomorrow.

"Mark let's get you back upstairs in your room. Hopefully if the doctor sees how you are doing we get can get you checked out early," Roxy said.

We hugged every one of our friends as they slowly started leaving the room to head to their homes. After hugging and talking with everyone, Nick and I decided that we would stay in the hospital for as long as we need to. We knew we didn't want to leave Aaron's side.

Chapter Two

AARON WAKE UP

When we walked into the room, we saw Aaron hooked up to a tube for his breathing. His eyes were closed. Wires were everywhere. It felt as though someone punched me in the gut. The wind was knocked out of me. My sweet boy is just lying there. I felt completely broken.

I walked slowly toward Aaron as he was lying there, "Hey sweet boy. If you can hear me, please know that we are here for you. I'm going to stay with you all night. I'll put on some worship music too. I know how you love worship music...my sweet...my sweet boy."

Nick gently rubbed my back. He always knows what I need when I can't express what I need. I tell Nick was trying to be calm, but I know on the inside this was breaking his heart. Aaron was our rainbow baby. We had a miscarriage before getting pregnant with Aaron. He was our miracle. The thought of losing our boy was unbearable.

Nick softly began to speak, "Hey, buddy. I know you're strong. You're stronger than your old man. But, listen, we need you, buddy, okay? We need you to be a fight
er. We are here for you. Whatever you need, mom and I are here. I'm staying here tonight too. Landon and Lucy are staying at Mimi and Papa's tonight. I'm sure they are worried about you too. They need their big brother."

Nick and I both looked at each other. Then, without saying a word, we both knew what we were thinking...

How on earth did we get here?
How is this even happening?
How will we tell Aaron that his best friend is now with Jesus?

I prayed silently with tears continuing to flow down my cheeks. "God, please save my baby...my sweet baby boy. My heart is aching more than I can take. This is overwhelming. God please...please..."

The next morning Nick and I were both so exhausted. We were in and out sleeping in the room and walking the halls out of frustration about the situation and anxiousness. We would take turns holding Aaron's hand. I combed my fingers gently in his hair. The nurses were giving him incredible care and were in and out of the room all night. So, we both felt like we only got an hour or two of sleep.

I had fallen asleep again by Aaron's bed while holding his hand. I woke up to hearing a gentle knock at the door and sniffling. It was Erica. She had a boot on her leg and crutches. As I rubbed my eyes to attempt to wake up, Erica immediately was crying about everything. Nick and I hugged her.

"I know sweet girl. I know. This is a lot. We are so glad that you and Tory are okay. We are believing that God will give us a miracle for Aaron too," I said softly.

Nick smiled and said, "How are you feeling this morning, kiddo? What did the doctor say about your concussion and your leg?"

Erica responded, "The doctor said that I have to take it easy for a while. I have to wear this boot on my leg, and I'm scheduled to get a cast in a couple of days. Then I'll wear that for about four to six weeks. But the doctor said that I should be okay and make a full recovery. This all happened so fast. I am still in shock over it to be honest. I can't believe Aaron is just lying here. I hate this. I want to do something, and I feel so hopeless about it all...Blake...Jean..."

I put my arm around Erica and said, "I know it. We all are in shock over it. To be honest, I cried myself to sleep last night. I hate seeing Aaron like this. I hate everything about what happened. But somehow... somehow Erica, I know God isn't going to waste any of it. I truly believe that. I believe that God is using Blake right now to help save several lives. I believe God is healing you, Tory, and Aaron. But I do understand the struggle of feeling hopeless in all of this. We've just got to place our trust in the Lord. All of this is in His hands...all of it."

Nick walked up to me and gently started rubbing my back. He knew it took everything in me to give Erica encouragement when I felt discouraged and exhausted.

"Here Erica why don't you go ahead and sit with Aaron a little while. Charlotte and I will go get some coffee in the cafeteria and get a little break. Is that alright?" Nick asked.

"Yes sir, that's fine. I'll sit with Aaron," Erica replied.

Nick gently took my hand and led me to the doorway. When we walked towards the door, we both turned and took another look at Aaron. What we both saw in this moment was truly precious. Erica started stroking Aaron's hair softly. Just like I have always done. We could both see the love that Erica has towards Aaron. It blessed us both to see that.

We then heard Erica gently start to sing, "Amazing grace...how sweet...how sweet...the sound..."

Nick gently put his hand on the small of my back and sweetly guided me out the door. He could sense that if he didn't guide me out the door, I'd never leave.

He softly said, "How does a coffee sound? They might even have some of that fancy boujee coffee you like and good grub in the cafeteria. My buddy Kevin from middle school is the head cook here. He said his goal is to change the way people see hospital cafeteria food. It's good. Some of the guys from my division come down here to eat sometimes when they're on duty."

I looked at Nick and smiled. He's always trying to cheer me up. I know he's hurting just as much as I am, yet he wants to make sure that I'm okay and taken care of. I just love him so much. I honestly don't know how I got blessed with this man of mine.

"Yes babe. That sounds good. It was sweet watching Erica with Aaron. Did you see how she stroked his hair like I do? Then she started singing Aaron's favorite hymn. I almost started bawling my eyes out when I saw that," I replied.

"Yep. I saw that. That's why I tried getting you

out of the room as fast as I could." Nick said with an ornery half-smile.

Sometimes Nick is fluent in sarcasm. Usually, it makes me laugh, but he just got a small half-smile from me this time. I knew he was trying to comfort me and distract me. We went in the cafeteria and got some food and sat down at an empty table that was away from everyone else. We both just wanted to be alone for a little bit. We needed to catch our breath and just simply sit without having to answer anyone's questions. We were both still in shock from it all. Nick sees stuff like this all the time, but when it's your own child...it's just different.

I saw Nick perk up with a look in his eye. I knew this look. It's the look that he gives when he notices that something is wrong or that someone isn't right.

"Babe, what's going on?" I asked.

Nick replied, "The news is here."

I started having chest pain and it was hard to breathe, "Are you freaking kidding me? I can't do this babe. I can't do this right now. Why are they here? Why do they have to do this rig...righ...right...now?"

I passed out in my chair and fell on the floor. I never had a panic attack like this, but this was the worst one yet. But, of course, I didn't realize I was having a panic attack at the time. Nick was in absolute

24

panic. All I heard was, "Oh my gosh babe! We need a doctor now!" I woke up to lights in my eyes and I saw Dr. Miller, a nurse, Nick, Roxy, and Mark looking at me. They had me sitting in a bed in the ER.

I slowly put my hand up by my head and said, "What's going on? What happened?"

"Charlotte, I believe you had a panic attack. Nick informed me of what happened and that's what I believe it to be. I want to run a couple of tests to make sure. I understand your situation, so I don't want to keep you all here any longer than you have to be. I know you want to be with Aaron, so I will make sure that we get you taken care of." Dr. Miller replied.

"Thank you doctor," Nick responded.

"Yes, thank you," I spoke softly.

Dr. Miller gently patted me on my shoulder and left the room. "Dang Charlotte, you just want all the attention don't you?" Mark said with an ornery grin on his face. Roxy then playfully hit Mark on his chest.

"Dude...Seriously though?" Roxy said while playfully rolling her eyes at Mark.

We all kind of giggled at Roxy and Mark's shenanigans. It was almost as if everything that we've gone through the past twenty-four hours was on pause mode.

25

The weight of the world wasn't there for a brief second...

But then reality set back in...

After they ran more tests, all my vitals came back normal. It was confirmed that I indeed had an anxiety attack. I felt so stupid. Why did I have to have an anxiety attack right now? My son is upstairs in a room, and he needs me. Yet here I am in the ER.
I took a deep breath and let out everything I was thinking. After that, I figured I could be transparent in front of Nick, Roxy, and Mark.

"You guys, I feel like an idiot. Why did I have an anxiety attack right now? Why is all of this happening? Why did we have to lose Blake and Jean? Why did God let this happen? I hate this. I hate this entire situation! Why babe? Why is our baby boy upstairs in a coma? I know God is good. I know He is. But I don't understand what God is doing right now! Also, why did the news crews have to be parked out front? Why are they all up in our business? I don't want them here at the hospital. It's already hard enough that we are in this damn situation. I'm sorry for cussing, it's just how I feel right now. I'm upset. I don't know how to fix it. Also, what about Erica? She's still up there with Aaron. Does she know that I'm here?"

Roxy got up from her chair and put her arms around me.

"Char, listen to me...first of all, none of us are judging you for cussing. We know you're upset and that's not you saying those things, it's the stress. Also, yes we checked on her, she's okay. Tommy and Julie are upstairs with her and Aaron right now. Secondly, you've handled all of this more gracefully than I could. Watching your faith in all of this is blessing so many people Char. The thing is sis, we don't know why things happen the way that they do...but we know ultimately Who is in control. God isn't caught off guard by any of this. God has been with all of us during everything."

"Roxy is right babe. I know you have felt like everyone has kept you going, but your faith helps mine every single day. Sweetheart, I hate this situation that we are in. But where I find peace in the middle of the storm is knowing that our Heavenly Father is right here with us and that I have you by my side. I'd be lost without you Char. I need you...always."

Nick then kissed my forehead and sat next to me on the hospital bed. Next, Dr. Miller's head nurse LeAnn came into the room.

"Mr. and Mrs. Johnson, I'm LeAnn and I'm Dr. Miller's head nurse. I'm going to go ahead and get you discharged so that you can go upstairs to be with Aaron."

"Thank you," I replied.

"Please tell Dr. Miller we said thank you for taking care of our family. God has really used her, you, and this amazing hospital staff to really help our family through one of the toughest valleys we've walked through." Nick humbly said.

LeAnn sweetly smiled, "It's an honor and privilege to serve you all. I want you all to know that I'm praying for you all. I am praying that God will do a miracle in Aaron's body."

Roxy and Mark hugged us, and Roxy looked at us both and said, "Hey Char and Nick, we would love to help you all out by taking the kids to our house for a couple of days. You all did that for us. Mark is going to be officially discharged tomorrow. So, it will work out perfectly for us. I know the next twenty-four to forty-eight hours are going to be crucial for Aaron and for you all. I'm sure your parents want to come and see Aaron and hug you both. I'm going to go pick them up tomorrow from your parent's Char."

Nick and I thanked and hugged Mark and Roxy goodbye. After getting discharged, we went upstairs. As we walked closer to Aaron's room we heard Tommy praying over Aaron. When we walked into the room, we saw the sweetest thing that I will forever hold in my memory. Tommy was praying and Julie and Erica had their heads bowed reverently before the Lord while they were holding hands with Aaron.

I couldn't help but start to cry. I think Tommy

heard me because he opened his eyes. He looked at Nick and I and we could see the love in his eyes for our family. After Tommy got done praying, we all said in unison, "Amen!"

Shortly after, Dr. Miller and some of her nurses walked into the room. There was another Dr. that we hadn't met before. Dr. Phipps was a neurosurgeon that wanted to come in and help Dr. Miller with further insight for what was about what the next step was for Aaron.

"Nick and Charlotte, my name is Dr. Walker Philipps. I had a similar case a couple of years ago. We were able to wake up the patient successfully. Dr. Miller asked if I could come help and assist with Aaron's case. Many doctors don't say this, but I am a praying man and I believe in miracles, from what I hear you all do too. I felt like God wanted me to help Aaron. So if it's alright with you folks, I'd love to help any way that I can."

We were all speechless. We all felt the presence of God in that hospital room. Nick and I looked at each other with tears in our eyes. We both took Aaron's hands and kissed him on the head.

Nick said, "Dr. Phillips, we'd love to have you on board. You see, this young man right here is our firstborn. He is strong...stronger than me. He's got a heart of gold like his mom. Anything you all can do to help our son is not only appreciated but welcomed. We

love him so much. This has all been a horrific night-
mare that we all want to wake up from."

I couldn't say anything. I was speechless. I was
worn. I felt empty. I had no strength left. All I could
do was go hug both Dr. Miller and Dr. Phillips with tears
going down my cheeks. As they both compassionately
smiled and hugged me, I felt peace.

Chapter Three

BELIEVING FOR A MIRACLE

"Here's the plan. Tomorrow evening, we are going to try and start waking Aaron up. We will do another brain scan in the morning to make sure that the swelling has continued to go down. After that, it's up to God Almighty and Aaron to see how he does. We are believing that this will go smoothly. There shouldn't be any permanent brain damage. We believe that Aaron will recover, but again...it's all in God's hands."

Erica, Tommy, and Julie all surrounded Nick and I and hugged us tight. "We are praying. We are believing that God is going to show off tomorrow. There is going to be a miracle!" Tommy said boldly.

Erica walked over to Aaron and gently kissed his forehead and the top of his nose...

She sweetly whispered in Aaron's ear, "Aaron, I love you. I know God is with you right now. Please Aaron, please fight with all that you have. We need you. You're my best friend. I love you."

Julie gently rubbed Erica's back. Julie and I both looked at each other and without saying a word, we knew what we were both thinking. It was such a sweet picture to see the love that Erica was showing Aaron.

After that, Nick and I hugged them all good-bye and told them that we would keep them updated. Shortly after Nurse LeAnn came in the room. She handed us a basket filled with snacks, bottled water, and a sack of clothes.

"Your friends Taylor and Zach dropped off some clothes and snacks for you all. They told me to tell you all that they are praying for you and that they love you all. I got some clean towels for you all and a few extra blankets and pillows. I know it's going to be hard to sleep tonight, but as best as you can, try to get some rest. Try to remember that God has this."

I hugged LeAnn and thanked her. Nick took the basket and started looking through it. It kind of made me giggle because he was like a kid on Christmas morning. I went over and sat by Aaron as Nick was picking out some of his favorite snacks.

Nick said with some excitement in his voice, "Oh yes! Zach got me those sour gummies that I love! I get these on almost every shift. I'm going to text him."

I smiled and then looked over at Aaron. I was watching him breathe in and out on the ventilator. My heart broke all over again. I couldn't help but cry. I tried not to show it, but I know Nick could see the tears.

I whispered softly in Aaron's ear, "Bub, it's momma. Listen, I need you okay? I need you. Daddy and I are so proud of you. We know you can fight this. You're so strong Bub. You're so very strong."

I kissed him on his cheek and stroked his hair. Then, Nick and I both took showers and went to sleep as best as we could. But, we knew Nurse LeAnn was right.

God is ultimately in control...

I woke up to Nick's voice. He was talking softly. At first I didn't know what he was saying, but then I realized he was talking to Aaron. I slowly turned towards Aaron's hospital bed and Nick was right there beside him. He was gently stroking Aaron's hair and praying over Aaron. He was asking God for a miracle for our son.

Then a few nurses came in and said, "We are going to take Aaron in now for a brain scan. We will bring

33

him back in about forty-five minutes to an hour. We encourage you all to go and eat breakfast in the cafeteria. Today is going to be a big day. You all need to eat. The biscuits and gravy are phenomenal."

Nick kissed the top of Aaron's head and I climbed out of the hospital cot that they gave us to sleep on and went and kissed Aaron on his forehead.

"I love you, Bub. We love you so much no matter what happens today, sweet boy. We are so proud of you." I gently said.

After the nurses rolled Aaron's bed out of the room, Nick and I looked at each other and took a deep breath. We didn't even need to say anything. Instead, we said it all by simply looking into each other's eyes. Both of us were scared, but at the same time, we knew that God orchestrated such a fantastic team of doctors and nurses that have given us comfort and encouragement in one of the darkest moments of our lives.

Nick looked at me and smiled, "Well babe, let's go downstairs to eat some of those amazing biscuits and gravy the nurses were talking about. Honestly, when they said biscuits and gravy, I felt like God was letting me know that today was going to be a good day. I know that sounds weird, but my Grandma Kaye made biscuits and gravy at her house when I would go over there. It was always so comforting to me."

I responded, "Yep, let's go for it. Honestly, biscuits and gravy sound amazing right now. You know what I was thinking about when the nurses told us they were serving biscuits and gravy in the cafeteria?"

"What's that, babe?" Nick asked.

"I was thinking about when Aaron rode his bike for the first time. Remember when I told him that I would cook anything he wanted if he would just go for it and try to ride his bike past the big willow tree down by the end of our driveway? But instead, Aaron looked at me with his superhero outfit on and boldly said, "Momma get ready to put the oven on! I'm gonna have some biscuits and gravy! Oh yeah!"

Nick laughed, "Wow, babe you know what, I do remember that! I was asleep because I was on night shift then. You were determined to get him to learn to ride his bike that week. Man, he talked about those biscuits and gravy all day long!"

We both laughed together as we walked toward the cafeteria. It felt good thinking about a sweet memory that we both held dear about Aaron. We were greeted by Roxy, Mark, Zach, Taylor, Keith, Tracey, Jordan, and some of the other officers that we've grown to love and be close to. They all hugged us, and it was such a blessing to see their faces.

Nick said, "Wow! Look at this crazy crew! Boy are we happy to see you all. We were just about to indulge on some biscuits and gravy. We'd love for you all to join us."

They all agreed, and we spend the next forty-five minutes or so, just enjoying their company. Jordan was telling us all about his date with Dr. Stephens and how they were going to go out again. Zach and Taylor talked about our farm and how the animals were doing. Zach said that Oreo took his wallet out of his pocket and ran with it. Their kids thought it was the best thing ever.

Mark was talking about how he was officially discharged. He was recovering faster than they initially expected. He just needed to take it easy. He was on administrative leave, so he said that he was just going to focus on getting better and stronger until they would release him to go back to work. Tracey and Keith were talking about how Tracey decided that she would run for Mayor. She was tired of how the current Mayor didn't support the men and women in blue. She wanted to make positive changes in our community.

It was so lovely just listening to everyone. It helped my mind shift from our current situation and helped me focus on everyone's situation. I can't believe the past week we've had. First, the shootout and Mark got shot. Second, we finally got Violet to go out with Will. And now this. I feel like I'm in the middle of a Rom-Com-Drama.

Nick's alarm went off on his phone. He said, "Char, it's time to get back upstairs. I bet they are close to being done with Aaron's scan. We thanked everyone for coming and hugged everyone.

Then Nick and I made our way upstairs. When we walked into the elevator, no one was in the elevator.

Nick turned towards me and hugged me. He said, "Char, no matter what happens today, we have each other. We will lean against each other. God has brought our family through some tough situations before. He will be faithful to do it again."
I smiled and he gently pulled my chin up to kiss him. He wrapped his arms around my waist and pulled me towards him.

He gave me another kiss and said, "Okay Mrs. Johnson, let's do this."

As we walked toward Aaron's room, we held each other's hands tight. We knew that we were walking into the unknown. We didn't know what would happen. We believed and prayed for a miracle, but we didn't know what the day would look like. Either way, we knew that it would change our lives forever. This entire situation has changed our lives forever.

We walked into Aaron's room, and it was empty. We wondered why Aaron wasn't in the room yet, but we patiently waited. About ten minutes passed, and then we heard a bed being pushed down the hallway. We knew that it was Aaron and his nurses. When they rolled Aaron's bed into the room, both nurses had smiles on their faces. Nick and I looked at each other; there must be some good news.

Nurse Amy said, "Well, Nick and Charlotte, we can't say too much right now; the doctor will be in shortly to talk with you all. But you all should know that the news is good news. Aaron is a fighter. God has His hands on him, that's for sure."

Nick and I both looked at each other with tears in our eyes. I gently squeezed Nick's hand. We knew at that moment that Aaron was going to be okay. This word of hope about Aaron was the word we needed. It was almost as if a huge weight had been instantly lifted.

When the doctor came in Nick and I couldn't wait to hear what he had to say, "Good morning Mr. and Mrs. Johnson. As you both know, we did a brain scan on Aaron. I have good news; the swelling has gone down to normal. Honestly, I haven't seen anything like this before. The scan this morning was almost as if Aaron had never been in an accident. The bruise on his brain was completely gone. There's no other way to say this...God did a miracle in Aaron. We are going to go ahead and start the process of waking him up. We will probably do this in about an hour or so. If you'd like to have family come up here, you're welcome to. However, I know you all have a huge support system. I'd encourage you all just to start with family for now. That way Aaron doesn't get too overwhelmed when he wakes up. Later on, though please feel free to invite your friends to come say hello to Aaron."

Nick and I couldn't help it; we both started laughing and hugging each other. I even ran and hugged the doctors and nurses! God did a miracle in Aaron. We both thanked the doctor, then we immediately called my parents and Nick's parents. We told them to come up to the hospital and asked them to go ahead and bring Lucy and Landon up to the hospital with them. We felt it was important for them to be here for their big brother.

Nick's parents were the first to arrive. When they walked into the room, Nick's parents started tearing up. They both hugged us and went over to Aaron and kissed him on his cheeks.

My parents walked in shortly after with Landon and Lucy. My parents teared up and went to kiss Aaron on his cheeks too. Landon and Lucy both looked shocked. Lucy came up and looked hesitant to even look at Aaron. Landon looked at his big brother lying in the hospital bed, and I could see the heartbreak in his eyes.

Nick trying to be strong for everyone said, "Well, we have good news everyone. The doctor said that God did a miracle in Aaron. The brain scan not only showed that Aaron doesn't have swelling on his brain, but the bruise on his brain is completely gone. The doctor said that Aaron's brain looks like he never even was in an accident."

As our parents, all in unison were thanking the Lord for healing Aaron, I looked over at Lucy, and I could tell she wanted to say something.

"What is it, Tootie?" I asked.

Lucy softly spoke with tears down her rosy cheeks, "Momma, do you think Aaron knows Blake is in Heaven now?"

I took a deep breath and said, "Baby girl, I don't know if he knows or not. But let's not tell him that right when he wakes up, okay? It will be a lot for Aaron to take in when he wakes up. So we've got to be as gentle as we can."

Landon walked over to Lucy and said, "It will be okay, sis. We know where Blake is. He's with Jesus. Can you imagine what he is seeing right now? I bet it's amazing. But, of course, knowing Blake, he is probably telling Jesus all his corny dad jokes."

Nick and I looked at each other, and we looked at Landon. We were so proud of him and how he was trying to step up and comfort his sister. We all circled Aaron and prayed together shortly after the doctor came in.

Chapter Four

OUR NEW NORMAL

"Hey folks, I'm Dr. Phillips. I'm one of the neurosurgeons here. Dr. Miller is going to join us here in a few minutes. We will then start the process of waking Aaron up. I want to go over a few things to expect. When waking someone up from a medically induced coma, it takes time for them to wake up. Think of it like a light switch that has a dimmer. It doesn't just happen automatically. It's a gradual process before the light is on. Also, we've got to keep a close eye on Aaron's lungs because of the breathing tube. We also want to pay attention and ensure there are no blood clots. Aaron will probably stay in the hospital for another three to five days so that we can keep a close eye on him. I've already said this to Mr. and Mrs. Johnson, but I'm a praying man. I know God is doing miracles in Aaron right now. I'm expecting Aaron to make a full recovery."

I looked over at our parents; there wasn't a dry eye in the room. We were all filled with great anticipation for Aaron to wake up. We just wanted to look into his beautiful blue eyes again and hear his voice. A slight panic came over me in thinking about explaining that Aaron's best friend was gone. Would Aaron wake up in a panic? Would Aaron be in denial of what happened? Would he remember what happened? There was just a flood of thoughts going through my mind. I think Nick could sense that I was starting to get a little anxious.

He started rubbing my back, and he whispered in my ear, "It's okay, Char. It's all going to be okay. God will give us the words we need. God will guide us on what to do for Aaron. I love you. You're an amazing mom and wife."

Dr. Miller came into the room and said, "Good morning, everyone. I'm Dr. Miller. We are about to start the waking-up process. I want you all to know that we are praying and believing for a miracle for Aaron today. God has already done amazing things. Are you all ready to get this process started?"

I cleared my throat, "Yes, ma'am. We are ready."

Dr. Miller responded, "Okay, so something to remember before we wake him up, try to keep things lighthearted. Try to be calm. Aaron has been through a traumatic event. He will need you all to help him through it."

All our family were holding hands. As they took the tube out and started the process, we were completely silent. We were all just staring at Aaron. We wanted so badly just to hear his voice. Finally, we slowly began seeing signs of Aaron waking up. It didn't happen as quickly as we'd hoped, but our baby boy was waking up.

Landon tapped Nick and said, "Dad look!"

Aaron was starting to move his fingers. A few more minutes went by, and Aaron started to open his eyes. He had a look on his face that was sad but peaceful. He began to try and talk, but his throat was sore. His voice wasn't very strong, but I could tell he was trying to tell us something.

Nick and I walked closer to him. "Mom and Dad, I'm sorry."

Nick and I had tears of joy rolling down our cheeks. But, of course, the first thing out of Aaron's mouth was that he was sorry.

I combed my fingers gently through his hair, "Bub, it's okay. It's okay, sweetheart. We love you so much."

Aaron tried to say something else, but it was

hard for him. We wanted to encourage him so that he didn't have to speak. So we told him to take it easy, and he could talk to us later. But he was determined. He wanted all of us to hear what he had to say. Boy, he's stubborn like his momma and daddy.

Aaron put his hand up to his throat and said, "I was there with Blake. I saw Him, momma. I saw Jesus. Jesus said it was Blake's time to be with Him, but I needed to stay here. My time wasn't done yet; He has stuff for me to do."

All of us immediately started weeping. Wow. Our baby boy saw Jesus! Not only did he see Jesus, but he saw Blake go with Jesus. My heart was immediately at peace. We all took turns hugging Aaron.

Dr. Miller overheard what Aaron had told us. With tears in her eyes and a smile on her face, she said, "Aaron, I'm Dr. Miller. I want you to know that you are a strong young man. God has His hands on you. We will keep you here for a few days just to monitor you, okay?"

Aaron smiled at her and gave her a thumbs up. We couldn't help but giggle at his response. That boy always knows how to make us smile.

Aaron gently spoke, "Dad and Mom, what about Erica and Tory? Are they okay?"

Nick said, "Yeah, buddy, they are both okay.

Erica has been up with you quite a bit. She's been worried about you. Everyone is going to come up later if you'd like them to. If you don't, that's okay too. It's up to you, buddy."

Again, Aaron smiled and gave us a thumbs up.

"I missed you, bro, but you're still a nerd," Landon said with an ornery grin.

Aaron stuck his tongue out at Landon and stuck up his pinky finger, and smiled. This was something that the boys had done since they were younger. They thought that the pinky finger was the middle finger. So, they would hold up their pinky fingers and toes, thinking they were shooting each other the bird. Usually, I'd get onto them for doing this, but I let it slide this time.

Lucy sweetly said, "God did a miracle for Aaron, didn't He? God gave us all a miracle."

Nick hugged Lucy and said, "Yes, baby girl, God gave us all a miracle."

My parents and Nick's parents hugged Aaron, Nick, and me goodbye. Landon went over to Aaron, and they did their secret handshake. Lucy went over and hugged her big brother. The kids, of course, gave Nick and me a big hug. Then my parents took Landon and Lucy over to Mark and Roxy's house to spend the night there.

"We love and appreciate you all for coming and helping us with the kids. Char and I are thankful for our family." Nick said as they all were leaving.

After they all left, Nick and I went over to Aaron, and we both sat down on the bed with him.

I looked at Aaron and said, "Bub, do you feel like having more company? I know Mark and Roxy want to be here, but they will give Mimi and Papa a break. So, Landon and Lucy will be hanging out there for a day or two. I know Erica is ready to come and see you. People from church want to see you. All the guys and gals at the police department want to come to see you. What do you think? We will respect what you want, bud. Just let us know."

Aaron said softly, "Sure...sure, mom, that will be alright. But first, can I tell you and dad what happened? I just feel like I owe you all an explanation of why things happened the way they did."

Nick gently tapped, "Bud listen, we kind of know what happened. You don't have to talk about that right now. As far as I'm concerned, you have been through enough. Are mom and I going to be a little more hesitant to let you drive after all this? Yeah, probably. Just because we almost lost you, kiddo. It's one of the scariest and hardest things we've been through. You are just so special to us. But please don't feel like you must go into what happened right now."

Aaron looked at us intently, "I appreciate that, dad, I do, but I really feel like I want to get this off my chest before everyone comes. Blake and I were on our way to the varsity basketball game. We were talking about how we hoped Coach would see our dedication and it would help us...help...help us be on varsity next year. Blake has...had this huge crush on Tory and begged me to switch seats with him...We were kind of arguing about it because I told him that you all said no one else could drive my car. He knew the rules. He wasn't trying to disobey your rules; he just wanted to impress Tory..."

Aaron took a deep breath and continued, "I finally went ahead and did what he wanted. Before I knew what had happened, I saw headlights coming right at us. I remember Blake shouting, "Jesus!" Then... then that's when I realized we were in trouble. I turned my head away and made eye contact with Erica, and I could see the terror in her eyes. Then that's when everything went dark for a minute. I saw a bright light, and Blake and I were with Jesus. Blake smiled at me, and Jesus said, "It's not your time yet, Aaron. I've got more for you to do. I'll come to get you when it's time." I saw Blake smile so big as he looked at Jesus, and then I woke up. I was trapped in the car. That's when I heard the firefighters working on getting me out of the car. That's all I remember. Then I woke up and I was here...Mom and Dad, are Erica and Tory okay? What happened to the car that hit us? I thought I saw Miss Jean from the church in the car next to us. But I wasn't sure if that was her or not. Is she okay?"

Nick and I were just in awe of what our son had just told us. We both couldn't help but cry tears of joy and sorrow. Joy because of our son's amazing experience and knowing that Blake was with Jesus. Sadness because we missed Blake and we were about to explain what happened to Jean. Grief is hard to understand at times. As Nick and I just sat there speechless, I think Aaron was wondering what we were thinking.

"Mom...Dad...are you all going to say anything? Are you okay?"

Nick gently tapped him on his arm, "Yes, bub. I think mom and I are just in awe of what you told us. To be honest with you, bud, what I'm about to tell you isn't going to be easy to hear...It appears that Miss Jean sacrificed herself for you all. Fred Duncan was the one that caused the accident. He was driving while drunk, and his truck was headed right towards you all. Jean must have seen what was about to happen, and she tried to take the brunt of the hit. She was killed instantly. I'm so sorry that you lost Blake. I've lost dear friends too. It's hard. There are no words. I guess I'm in awe because I haven't had the amazing opportunity to escort any of them into the arms of Jesus. That's awesome! What was it like, bud? What was Jesus like?"

Aaron, just taking it all in, responded, "Dad, you already know. You walk with Jesus every day. But, wow, I can't believe Miss Jean did that. That was brave of her."

Nick sweetly smiled, "Yes, it was brave of her. I'm forever grateful for what Jean did. But, bud, I know I walk with Jesus daily...I just mean, like, what did He look like? Did you see Heaven too? I am just curious."

"Honestly, Dad, Jesus is indescribable. His love is what I remember the most. All I felt was unbelievable love. A love that I haven't experienced here. Although, I've experienced a sliver of that love through you all, our family, Erica, and friends. The love of Jesus is so pure and overwhelming. Honestly, I didn't want to leave His presence."

"Wow, bub. I've got goosebumps! That is amazing! I know we can't even think of this right now, but eventually, I hope you'll share that with our church. I think your story could help inspire people." I replied.

Nick smiled at me, "Yes, I agree with Mom. Your story will help inspire people. Oh, bub, I had Keith grab your cell phone from your car. Grandma and Grandpa brought a charger, and I've been charging your phone. There's a huge crack in the screen, but it still works. You've been receiving a lot of text messages. Would you like me to try to read them to you? Or do you want to try and look at your phone to see the texts? If you look at your phone and get a headache, let's take a break. Dr. Miller did say that you need to be protective of yourself for a week or so. After that, you've got to ease back into the normal day-to-day things."

"Thanks, dad; I might wait a little bit. I know

that Blake texted me, and there are a few voicemails from him. Even with all that I know and the opportunity to see him with Jesus, it's hard. I miss him. He is... he...he was like my brother."

I gently stroked Aaron's hair. "That's okay, bud. Do you need more time? That's okay if you are. If you need to wait to see everyone, that's more than okay."

Aaron took a sip of water and cleared his throat. "I don't mind seeing everyone. But if it's alright, I'd like to try and take a shower before I see anyone. I would like to see Erica first."

Sure, bud, no problem. Grandma and Grandpa brought you some clean clothes too. So you go ahead and take a shower. Mom can call Erica's parents, and they can come up here.

While Aaron was in the shower, Nick and I were just sitting in silence for a few minutes. Both of us were still trying to take everything in that Aaron had just told us. What he remembered and how scared he must have been right before the accident when he saw headlights coming towards the side of his car. And

"Thank you, babe. I appreciate you more than you know. I am so grateful that God picked you to be my husband. I don't know what I'd do without you, Nick."

I kissed Nick and then kissed his cheek and hugged him. There's nothing better than melting into hearing Blake shout, "Jesus!"

"Babe...babe...babe...Char..."

Nick looked at me, and I must have been zoning out for a second because I didn't hear anything; he said, "Char, are you alright? I've been trying to get your attention, and you were just zoning out."

"I'm sorry, babe, I was just thinking about every-thing. I guess I was playing out that entire scenario in my mind. But, wow. I don't think I can get it out of my mind—all of it. Hearing Aaron's perspective and what he saw...what he heard...how scared he was. I'm just... I'm just trying to calm down from it. I guess hearing all of it just made me, in a way, relive every kind of emo-tion that we've had with all this. Is that stupid?"

Nick took a chair that was in the room and put it directly in front of me. He gently grabbed my chair and scooted as close as possible to me. He gently pushed my curtain bangs out of my eyes, and he gently start-ed to kiss me.

"Babe, first of all, you're never stupid. Nothing you do is stupid. So please don't say that again. Sec-ondly, sweetheart, it's normal to feel what you're feel-ing. Finally, Babe, we have all been through trauma. It will take time, but God will help all of us as we heal. We have each other to lean on. We are all in this together, babe."

this man's arms. The way he wraps his strong arms around me makes me feel so safe.

"I'm going to go get a coffee and maybe something to snack on in the cafeteria. I need to stretch my legs a little bit. Then, I'll call Tommy and Julie and tell them that Aaron would like to see Erica."

Nick responded, "Okay, babe. You alright to go downstairs alone? I can go with you if you want me to."

"It's alright, babe; I just need to take a minute."

"Alright, Char, I understand. I'll just hang here and let Aaron know that you're calling Tommy and Julie." Nick responded.

After I left the room, I started to pray silently...

"Lord, thank you for being here for all of us in this situation. Thank you for being so faithful. Thank you, God, for being with Blake and Jean. I know they are both with you. Help us, God move forward and find a new normal. Things are going to be different. They are already different. God, help us focus on you when we go through grieving. I know it will be hard on all of us, especially Blake and Jean's family and Aaron. Amen."

As I continued to walk towards the elevator, I walked past a room. I couldn't help but notice this family that was there. They were all crying. I could tell that their loved one had passed away. My heart ached for them. That very well could have been our family. That's what Blake's family and Jean's family are going through. I felt humbled at that moment.

As I walked closer to the elevator, I stopped and decided to go ahead and call Julie. I told her they could come up to the hospital whenever they would like to. Aaron wanted to see Erica.

After getting my coffee and chips, I headed back upstairs towards Aaron's room.

I felt guilty because I was listening to Aaron and Nick's conversation, but I waited out in the hall because I could tell that they were having a heart to heart.

"Dad, how did you know that mom was the one?"

"Honestly, bub, I know some may say that this isn't possible, but I knew the moment I saw your mom that she was the one for me. She was beautiful, but I watched how she was with people. Her sweet and gentle heart captivated me. I wanted to be around her all the time. She made me laugh a lot. I knew that I wanted her to be my wife. So, after I met her, I prayed, and God gave me the thumbs up, so I asked her to marry me. So now here we are; I love your mom more now than ever. She's my everything. Just wondering, bub, why do you ask?"

"Dad, I know I'm still in high school, but I know that Erica is the one for me. This accident gave me perspective. I want to ask Erica to marry me someday, dad. After graduation. Maybe even right before graduation. I want to ask her. What do you think about that?"

"Buddy, listen, Erica is amazing. When you were in the coma, your mom and I saw Erica stay right by your side. She sang your favorite worship songs. She prayed with you. I know mom feels this way; we would love to have Erica be our daughter-in-law. Remember, though; you have to ask her father and mother's permission first. If I were you, I'd wait until after graduation or at the earliest...graduation night."

"Oh, yes, sir. I will. I'll let you all know when I ask them."

I then walked into the room. "What are you boys talking about?"

"Mom, I know you heard us."

"Wait, how did you know?" I said, surprisingly.

Aaron laughed and said, "Mom, dad, and I saw your foot sticking out by the door."

"Oh, my stars! Why didn't y'all say anything?" I asked.

Nick started laughing, "Babe, listen, you aren't very discreet. I saw that pretty foot of yours sticking out by the door. But I was just gonna let it go. Aaron saw it, too, and pointed. I winked at him. We knew you were trying to be respectful and wait for us to get done."

I went over and sat on Nick's lap. "You boys sure are ornery; I'll tell you that much."

Not long after Erica came in, she paused at the door. Aaron looked over at her, and I saw the love in their eyes. She walked over to Aaron and laid next to him on his hospital bed. She put her head on his chest. They didn't even say anything at first. She just wanted to hug him.

"Hey, pretty girl," Aaron said.

"Hey." Erica smiled.

Not long after, Tommy and Julie came in. They looked over at Aaron and Erica and smiled.

"Hey Aaron, it's so good to see you! We've been praying like crazy. Everyone at the church is asking about you. How are you feeling?" Tommy asked.

"Doing a little better, sir. The doctor wants me to try to walk around a little bit with my crutches this evening. I broke my tibia. The doctor said that it could take four to six months to heal. I'm praying it will be more like four months at the most. But I'm believing for God to heal it."

"Aaron, we are so glad you're alright. We've been praying, sweetie. I know God has been right by your side. But, Charlotte, have they said when he will be going home yet?" Julie asked.

"The doctor said it should be in the next day or two. It would be amazing to get to go home tomorrow." I responded.

"This hospital is top-notch. They have gone above and beyond to help our family. Even when Char had to go to the ER, they got us checked and discharged quickly so we could come back and be with Aaron." Nick said.

"Wait...what? What happened to mom?" Aaron asked with concern.

I looked over at Nick. I could tell that Nick had one of those moments that we all have. Where the words come out, and you don't realize what you're say-ing until after you're done saying it. Lord knows I've been there more than a time or two.

I smiled and patted Nick's arm, "It's okay, babe. Yeah, so I had an anxiety attack. It's alright. No big deal. I'm okay, so no need to worry."

Aaron looked at me, and I could tell that his

heart hurt for me. He hated that I had an anxiety attack. The last time I had one was when Nick went on his first foot chase a couple of years back. Aaron was younger, but I could tell he instantly remembered that moment when I had that anxiety attack.

"Mom, I'm so sorry."

I walked toward Aaron, "Oh bub, it's okay. Don't you worry about me. I'm alright."

"Bub, I'm sorry. I didn't mean to catch you off guard. Honestly, I'm just a little tired. I think I will go down and get a coffee in the cafeteria. Tommy, Julie, and Char, if it's alright with you all, let's go ahead and give these two a few minutes." Nick said.

We all agreed and went downstairs to stretch our legs, get some more coffee, and allow Aaron and Erica to talk. They haven't gotten to speak since Aaron has come out of his coma. So, we all knew they wanted to say things about what happened that night. I knew that Aaron would probably tell her what he told us. Plus, Nick and I always love talking with Tommy and Julie. Not only are they dear friends of ours, but we just love and respect them a lot. I love working with Tommy at the church. There's never a dull moment there, that's for sure.

As we went downstairs, Tommy and Julie were sweetly just talking with us and trying to start a conversation that had nothing to do with our situation.

Nick and Tommy, of course, had to have their battle of "dad jokes." Of course, Julie and I always just laugh because we think they are cute. But, sometimes...okay, most of the time, when the guys are making their dad jokes, what they think is funny is funnier than the jokes they tell.

When we went down to the cafeteria, we found a table in a quiet spot. Nick and I looked at each other, and I nodded at him. We both knew that we wanted to share what Aaron had told us. We couldn't keep it in any longer.

"Go ahead, babe; I can tell you want to tell them," Nick said.

Tommy and Julie were both adamantly looking at us. They wanted to know what I was about to say.

"What is it, Char?" Julie asked.

"When Aaron woke up and started getting his thoughts together, he told us what happened. He talked about how the accident occurred from his point of view. Not only did he tell us about the accident, but what amazed Nick and I was what happened right after the accident..." I paused.

"Charlotte, what happened right after the accident?" Tommy asked with great anticipation.

"Aaron said that everything went black when the

truck hit their car. Then he said that he saw Jesus and Blake. Jesus told him that it wasn't his time and he had more for Aaron to do. He said that Blake looked at him and smiled, and there was overwhelming peace. When he woke up, he knew Blake was with Jesus."

When I was saying all of this, I looked at Julie and Tommy, who were both in awe. Julie had tears going down her cheeks. They both were just completely amazed.

I smiled and said, "I know Aaron will probably tell you all when he's ready. But I couldn't hold it in any longer. I had to tell you guys."

"Charlotte, I'm so glad you did tell us. Wow. To imagine what Aaron got to see is truly amazing. I know it will be a while, but when he's ready, I'd love for him to share that with our congregation at church." Tommy said.

"We will pray about that, brother. I know it's going to be a process for Aaron to heal. But knowing him, he's a lot like his mom in this way; he has no problems with sharing what God has done in his life." Nick replied.

"For now, do you all mind keeping this between us? I would love for Aaron to share his heart with you when he's ready." So I said to Tommy and Julie.

"No problem at all, Char, we completely understand that. We love you all. We love Aaron. Our Erica loves him too. That's something that God has shown us during all this is that her love for Aaron is genuine. It's not puppy love, but real authentic love. We love how he treats her too." Julie replied.

I hugged Julie, "Thank you, guys; we love and appreciate you so much. We love Erica too. She's so precious, and watching her and how she treated our boy made us realize how strong their love was. She didn't care if we were there; she was going to pray for Aaron and sing his favorite worship songs. It was the sweetest thing."

As we all made our way upstairs, I noticed Tommy and Nick making eye contact. Julie and I looked at each other confused. We knew they were up to something but had no clue what these two were about to pull. Nick smiled with a huge ornery grin when we got on the elevator.

He gave the nod to Tommy. Suddenly, Tommy started pushing every single floor button. So, on every floor we went to, the doors would open. When people saw the lit-up buttons, they looked at us with pure judgment. Some started laughing, but most of the looks given were looks of disapproval. Luckily, we weren't on the hospital's top floor; that would have been so embarrassing. Leave it to Nick and Tommy to do something this goofy. Honestly, it's exactly what I needed. I needed these shenanigans to help relax my overstimulated mind.

After getting to the room, Erica was still sitting on the bed with Aaron. They were laughing and just talking about ordinary things. I could tell Erica had been crying a little. I'm sure they talked about everything.

"Alright, baby girl, it's time to head home, okay? I'm sure Aaron needs some rest. We will bring you back tomorrow." Tommy said.

After they left, Nick and I asked Aaron what he wanted to eat. He wanted tacos, so naturally, we ordered his favorite ones and delivered them to the hospital. We knew he needed his strength before testing out his crutches. Aaron was so thankful, and he ate every single bite of the tacos. He did perfectly with his crutches too. I was so grateful when I watched my baby boy go down the hospital hallway with his crutches and Nick by his side. I was thankful that God gave us the gift of more time with our sweet boy.

However, of course, my flesh gets in the way. I'd be lying if I said I wasn't ready to go home. I missed looking out at our farm animals and being with Landon and Lucy. I missed my bathtub too. But even with all of that, I knew the bigger picture was that Aaron was here. His body is healing a little bit every minute. Honestly, I think I'm just exhausted. I'm ready to get this sweet boy of ours home. I'm ready to find our new normal.

Chapter Five

GOING HOME AND PANCAKES

The next morning, we woke up to the sound of Dr. Miller and Dr. Phillips coming into Aaron's room. It was kind of funny and embarrassing because Nick and I wanted to try and sleep next to each other, which really turned into us making a weird mega bed with a hospital chair and cot that they brought us. I couldn't get comfortable, so Nick told me to just lay on top of him. This, of course, was oblivious to Aaron because he was so worn out from trying his crutches and walking around last night.

So, when Dr. Miller and Dr. Phillips came into the room and saw Nick and me on top of each other, I was afraid other thoughts went through their minds. When we woke up, Nick and I smiled at the doctors, looked at each other, and popped up quickly. This, of course, startled Aaron and made Dr. Miller and Dr. Phillips laugh out loud!

"Just to clarify with everyone in the room, Char and I were not trying to get romantical..." Nick said.

Aaron interrupted, "Wait! What? Oh, my stars Dad! Mom! Seriously? I mean, I know you all are cuddly with each other and all, but seriously?"

Dr. Miller and Dr. Phillips couldn't help but fill the room with their laughter. This entire situation got way out of hand fast! Nick and Aaron started laughing, and I could feel that my face was as red as a strawberry. I was so embarrassed. I kind of giggled a little bit, but I was mortified. The doctors probably thought we were a hot mess. I wouldn't necessarily disagree with either of them on that.

Dr. Miller replied, "Well, it sure is exciting in here today, folks! Aaron, we heard from Nurse LeAnn that you did fabulous last night. That's amazing news. God truly did a miracle in you, young man."

"Yes, ma'am. I believe that with all my heart." Aaron smiled.

"All of Aaron's vitals look great. Dr. Miller and I both agree that we think Aaron can officially get discharged today. What do you think of that, Aaron?" Dr. Phillips asked.

"That sounds amazing, Sir. Thank you so much. Thank you for helping me." Aaron said in a soft voice as he held back tears.

"Thank you both so much. God used you both and your amazing team of nurses to help our son. I pray that God blesses you all double! Honestly, this has been one of the darkest moments of our lives. You all were a light in the darkness for our family. Can I give you all a hug?" I asked.

"Of course! Come on over here, sister!" Dr. Miller said with her arms wide open.

As we all hugged them and thanked them, we were all overjoyed. This situation could have turned out so differently.

"Nurse Kim will come into the room shortly with your discharge paperwork and prescriptions. Please stay in touch, and don't hesitate to call us if you all should need anything at all." Dr. Phillips said in a sincere tone.

After we were officially discharged, Nick went to get the car. Nurse Kim and I pushed Aaron down in a wheelchair to the hospital entrance. It seemed a bit surreal to me to see the entrance. It felt like we were in the hospital forever, and it was only almost a week. As weird as this may sound, I was almost having a flashback of when we left this hospital with Aaron after having him. I remember Nick and I drove so slowly. We were completely and utterly terrified. We didn't want anything to happen to our sweet baby boy.

When Nick pulled up, he rolled down the window and shouted, "Hey, party people, wanna hop in my ride?"

"Dad, I just can't with you right now," Aaron said as he laughed hysterically.

Nick always knows what to do to make Aaron smile. It always blesses my heart to see them interact with each other. How did I get so blessed to have this amazing man as my husband and this amazing young man who is now taller than me as my son?

"Alright, babe, let's get his stuff and head home. I'm ready to see our other two babies and all our animal babies. Also, I want pizza tonight. Does that sound good?" I asked.

Nick excitedly responded, "Yes! Babe, you read my mind! Pizza sounds freaking amazing right now. I mean, the hospital food was good, don't get me wrong. But Daddy needs some pizza ASAP!"

"Pizza sounds amazing right now. Not gonna lie. Are Landon and Lucy going to be there right when we get home?" Aaron asked.

"Yes, bub. Mimi and Papa are there now. Mimi texted me earlier and said that Lucy spent the entire evening creating signs for your door, and she cleaned

your room for you. She wanted to make sure her big bubba had clean sheets and that you could just go to your room and relax. Also, Landon wanted to try and make some of your favorite strawberry cake that Mimi makes. She helped him with the recipe. He also wanted to make sure the house was properly stocked with your favorite snacks. I know they both missed you like crazy. They were so worried about you. We all were."
I responded.

I felt Aaron from the backseat reach up to gently hold my hand. This blessed my heart so much. We did this on the way to school before he could drive. He and I would hold hands and pray together every day before school. I would always say, "Okay, bub, let me see your hand." He would always know that meant we were about to pray.

It's truly amazing the things you think about once something traumatic in our lives happens. We get a perspective shift. We realize the little moments shared with loved ones are so precious, valuable, and irreplaceable. We recognize how much value we place on things that, in the end, don't really matter. The sweet memories. The people in our lives matter. First and foremost, the relationship we have with the Lord matters. That's what really matters...everything else is just smoke...here today, gone tomorrow.

When we pulled down our street, I could hear a sigh of relief from the back seat. I could tell that Aaron was ready to be home. I know the car ride home was probably a bit triggering with everything that had happened. But, when we pulled into our driveway, what we saw next was a sweet picture that will forever be engrained in my memory.

My parents, Nick's parents, Landon, and Lucy were all holding signs in the front yard. At first, I wondered how long they all must have been standing outside, but then I remembered that we have the app on our phones that shared our location. Lucy always watches that app like a hawk when one of us leaves the house.

I looked in the rearview mirror, seeing Aaron's facial expression. He had a sweet smile on his face with a couple of tears going down his cheeks. I knew he was thinking how grateful he was to still be here. I'm sure he also felt guilty that he was still here and Blake wasn't. But I knew that Aaron had to go through this process of grief to heal, and we were going to be here for him to lean on.

As the car stopped, I could hear Aaron take a deep breath. Nick and I could tell that he just needed a second. So, we slowly got out of the car, and then we opened Aaron's car door for him. Nick went around to the trunk to pull out Aaron's crutches. As Aaron used his crutches to go toward the house, Nick's parents and my parents started clapping and cheering for Aaron. Landon and Lucy looked at each other and started in on the   celebration. We could hear Bowden and Zeus barking and all our cows, chickens, and goats. It felt so good to be home finally.

Aaron hugged everyone, and after our parents hugged and kissed Aaron, they all agreed that they weren't going to stay. Instead, they would let our kids and us have the evening to relax and adjust quietly at home. So after we waved goodbye, we all went inside. Landon and Lucy were so helpful and sweet. Landon helped Nick carry in all the balloons and flowers that Aaron received at the hospital. Lucy helped Aaron get comfortable in the recliner in the living room.

I went to my room to take a shower and change into my pajamas. After getting comfortable in my pajamas, I went out into the living room. Nick was playing on the ground with Bowden and Zeus. The kids were all laughing and enjoying the dogs being their crazy selves.

Lucy looked at me with excitement, "Mom, look at Bowden! He's trying to sit on dad's head! Isn't that hilarious? Dad said that Bowden smelled like the goats. I told him that he smelled like the goats earlier; Papa let Zeus out, and Zeus started chasing something that went into the barn. Bowden was concerned, so he ran after Zeus. It turns out that Zeus was chasing Oreo! Oreo had some of dad's work gloves, and Zeus was trying to chase her. Bowden was trying to retrieve dad's gloves! It was a whole thing! You should have seen Mimi and Grandma chase after the dogs. You would have peed your pants, mom!"

We all started laughing. The sound of laughter echoing in our home was something that my heart needed. Our home felt complete at this moment. We all decided to watch one of our favorite movies and eat popcorn together. There's nothing better than grabbing those big bulky soft blankets, fuzzy socks, pajamas, and movie theater popcorn. Lucy and Landon both sat on either side of me. They both said they just wanted to share my popcorn with me, but I knew they just needed me. I needed them too. Nick sat on the loveseat with Bowden and Zeus, and Aaron was comfortable on the recliner.

After the movie was over, Nick and I made sure that Aaron had everything he needed. I handed him the remote control and kissed him on his forehead. Nick and I then went upstairs to tuck Landon and Lucy in bed. We were intentional about spending a little bit of quality time with them to ensure they were okay. We had all been through so much.

We could tell that Landon was trying to be strong, but he was short with us. He was going through the motions like all of us were. Lucy was teary-eyed and expressed her hurt and confusion about everything. We tried to explain what we could, but we knew we wanted Aaron to share what he went through with them. We just wanted to comfort them both as best as we could.

Nick and I both bought three journals from the gift shop at the hospital. We wanted the kids to all journal how they were feeling. We wanted them to have a productive outlet to pour out their emotions and inner thoughts. So, Nick and I gave Landon and Lucy their journals and explained what they were for. They both were receptive to the idea, which we prayed they would. We were thankful that the journaling conversation with both of them went as well as it did.

When Nick and I headed downstairs to check on Aaron one more time, we heard some whimpering. When we saw what was going on, Zeus and Bowden were just being so gentle and licking Aaron and rubbing their head against him gently. Nick and I were amazed at how perceptive the dogs were to Aaron's situation. They weren't in their usual crazy form; they were being gentle and wanted to love on Aaron. Animals are amazing that way. After getting Aaron settled, Nick and I prayed with Aaron and hugged him.

"Goodnight, bub. Mom and I love you so much, dude. Even though you are a goober nugget."

"Yeah, yeah, goodnight Dad. Goodnight mom. Love you both."

"Goodnight, sweetheart. Try to get some rest, okay?"

"Okay, I'll try, mom. I love you both. Oh, mom, can you please get me some more water?"

"Sure bub." As I handed him his water, he gave

me another big hug.

Aaron softly said, "I love you mom."

"I love you too bub. Get some rest okay?"

Nick went ahead to take a shower and get settled for bed. While I got Aaron his water and made
sure the front door was locked. I then headed towards
the bedroom. Nick was still in the shower. I got my
favorite vanilla-scented lotion and put lotion on my
hands, arms, and feet. It felt so nice just getting to sit
on our own bed. When Nick got out of the shower, he
came into our bedroom with his towel around his waist.

"Hey, handsome." I winked at Nick.

"Hey, there, gorgeous. Are you happy to be
home?" He asked.

"Yes, I am, babe. Yes, I am. I'm so exhausted.
This bed feels so amazing." I replied as I sank into our
blankets.

"You know what also sounds amazing?" He said
in a flirtatious voice.

"Babe, you know I love me some you! But this
girl is completely exhausted. I promise tomorrow, I'll
give you some much-needed sexy time. Right now, I
just feel like I am worn and exhausted. I want to

snuggle with you and go to sleep, if that's okay. I adore you, though. You know that."

"Babe, I know. It's okay. Honestly, I figured that would be your answer because of everything. But you can't blame me for trying. I mean...you are pretty hot. Especially this morning when we were awakened from our slumberrrrr." He replied in a goofy voice while flirtatiously winking at me.

We both were laughing uncontrollably. We both were imagining the looks on our faces as the doctors came in to talk about discharging Aaron.

I turned towards Nick, "Babe, we are a hot mess. You know that, right? Like holy moly. I know the sweet Lord looks at us like, "Well, here these two goobers go again."

"Yep, babe, we are. But that's alright. That's the way I like it." I love you, Char."

Nick kissed me softly and held me close. I love just melting into his arms.

The next morning, we woke up to the sound of the dogs barking to go outside. I went ahead and got up so that Nick could sleep in a little bit. What I saw next was certainly unexpected...

I saw Roxy, Mark, and their kids, Anna and Sean, Taylor and Zach and their kids, Violet and Will, Keith,

Tracey, Jordan, Jessica and Toby, and Tommy, Julie, and Erica were all outside. They were all setting up long tables and chairs. As I watched what was going on, Lucy came running down the stairs.

"Mom, go lay down. Or go do something. We are trying to make a special pancake breakfast outside. It's supposed to be a surprise!"

"Okay, baby girl, I'll just grab a quick cup of coffee, and then I'll go lay down. Where's Aaron?"

"Oh, I accidentally woke him up when I came downstairs earlier. I told him what was happening because he made me tell him, and he wanted to be sure to take a shower. So, he's using the guest shower now."

"Okay, Tootie, well, I'm going to go back to my bedroom for a little bit. What time do we need to go outside?"

Lucy looked at the kitchen clock, "Okay, what time is it? It's 8:30, so come outside at nine, okay, Mom? Bring Dad and Aaron too. Landon is already outside helping set up chairs."

So, as I went back into the bedroom, I sat down my coffee on the dresser. Then, I gently climbed into bed and snuggled next to Nick. Then, of course, I had to put my cold feet on him. Because...well...you know...I love messing with him.

Nick opened his eyes and shouted, "Oh wow! That's freaking cold! Babe! Why?!?"

I couldn't help but laugh. I guess I felt bad for waking Nick up like this, but I'll just have to make it up to him later.

"Babe, I'm sorry I just thought it would be funny."

"Yeah, Char, freaking hilarious. Why are your feet so cold, babe? Get some socks on those things."

He then proceeded to hug me and just held me in his arms. For a minute, I forgot that everyone was outside preparing pancakes. I also forgot that my hair looked crazy and that we were supposed to be outside soon. Then I remembered...

"Ummmm, babe..."

"What is it, Char?"

"Nick, we've got to start getting ready."

Nick looked a bit puzzled, "Get ready for what? Also, why didn't you call me babe? Am I in trouble or something?"

I giggled and gently kissed Nick's cheek, "Babe, everyone is outside right now. No, you're not in trouble. I'm just not awake. Momma needs more coffee."

"Like when you say everyone...who? The kids? I'm confused."

"No, babe, like literally everyone is here. They are all making a big pancake breakfast for the kids and us. They brought tables from the church and every-thing. Aaron is taking a shower, Landon is outside, and Lucy is heading outside to help. I only know about this because I woke up to let the dogs out and get a cup of coffee. Lucy ran downstairs and told me to go back into our room and explain what was happening. So, we need to get up and get ready quickly."

Nick responded with an ornery smirk, "Wow, that's sweet of them. I know you appreciate not hav-ing to cook this morning, too, huh, babe?"

"I knew right when you gave me that ornery smirk you would say something a bit smart-assy. I love you, babe. I think it's good for us to be encouraged by hanging with our friends and their families, don't you?" I asked.

"I do. I really do. I'm thankful for all of them. Our family and friends have gone above and beyond for our family. From taking care of the farm, and our kids, to bringing snacks and food to the hospital. They have all been our backbone through all of this. Let's get up and get dressed then, beautiful."

We got up and got dressed. As we walked out to the kitchen, we saw Roxy, Anna, and Violet getting a few rolls of paper towels and ice.

"Well, look at this ornery crew in our kitchen. What are y'all up to?" Nick asked.

"Well, we decided you all needed some pancakes this morning. Violet made her homemade blueberry and strawberry syrup. Will made his famous egg casserole. Anna made some blueberry muffins. Jordan said he wanted to bring the bacon. Keith and Tracey brought the fruit. And we all just brought a bunch of snacks and stuff for all of us to munch on. Y'all ready to see what we got?" Roxy asked.

"Let's go for it! Aaron, you almost ready, bud?" I asked.

"Charlotte, he's already outside. As we speak, he's sitting with Erica on the swing right now." Violet said.

As we all went outside, everyone started to cheer! They were all just excited to see all of us together. Erica was so sweet to help Aaron get down our front porch stairs. Bowden and Zeus were going crazy and chasing the goats. The sounds of the chickens and cows were just so relaxing. It was nice just simply to be. Lots of laughter and delicious food were icing on the cake.

I couldn't help it; I had to make a little announcement. So, I tapped my glass and said, "If y'all don't mind, I'd like to say something really quick. You all are so sweet to do this for us. We can't thank you enough for everything. We hope you all know how valuable each of you are to our family. We honestly don't know what we'd do without you all. Having you all to lean on and pray with has made all the difference in the world. Thank you from the bottom of our hearts."

We all spent a few hours together outside. We were all just enjoying each other, and the kids were all playing tag and hanging out. It was almost as if everything was going to be alright. We could finally breathe a little.

That's when my cell phone rang...

When I looked to see who was calling, it was Blake's mom's cell number. Nick saw who it was and looked at me with concern and sadness. It hit me like a ton of bricks. I felt like I got punched in the gut. I had so many thoughts flood my mind.

As I stood up, I went ahead and picked up the phone. Then, I walked away from all the tables and went up to my porch. As I sat in the swing, I took a deep breath and answered the phone.

"Hey Charlotte, it's Ummm... it's Trish...."

Chapter Six

BLAKE'S FUNERAL

I paused. "Hey, Trish...I'm just...I'm just at a loss for words. I have thought about you all every single day since the accident. I wanted to come by and see you. We just got home last night. Trish, my heart aches. I hate this. I hate all of it. I just...I just."

As I started to cry, I could hear Trish cry too. We both hated what had happened. We both wanted to change it. But unfortunately, there were no words that could be said to fix it.

I cleared my throat... "Trish, I can't imagine what you're feeling right now. I came close to knowing what you're feeling, but the strength you are displaying right now...honestly, there aren't any words to describe it. I know God is with you. Trish, I have to tell you something that Aaron told us when he woke up from his coma. He told us that he got to see Blake with Jesus. He said that Blake had a huge smile on his face and that Blake was so unbelievably happy to be with Jesus. I know I'm not doing Aaron's story justice right now. He can tell you more about it, but He did see him with Jesus Trish. He really did."

Suddenly, I heard a loud shout mixed with crying and laughter. I thought that maybe I had said the wrong thing, but I wasn't sure. I looked at Nick, and Nick could hear Trish.

He looked at me with concern and whispered, "What's happening?" I looked at him and shrugged my shoulders. I had no idea what was happening at this moment. Was Trish upset with what I said? Should I have kept this to myself? I was only trying to encourage her.

"Charlotte! Charlotte! What did you just say? Did you say that Aaron saw Blake with Jesus?"

"Yes, Trish...that's what I said. When Aaron was in his coma, Nick and I were trying to figure out how to break the news to Aaron that Blake had passed away. When Aaron woke up, he already knew that Blake was gone because he got to see Blake go with Jesus. Jesus looked at Aaron and told him that it wasn't his time yet. He still had work for Aaron to do."

"Wow, Char. I'm just...I'm speechless...how amazing is that? Aaron got to escort his best friend to Heaven...I'm in awe...Charlotte, listen. I've talked to God a lot lately. I am honestly still processing it all. But here's what I know to be true, even though I hate all of this. Even though I wish I could...I could...I could hug Blake and tell him how much I love him one more time. I just...I must hold onto the fact that God was with Blake that night. God was with all of those involved. When I got the call that Blake was gone, my heart sank. There are no words to describe the pain I felt...that I'm still feeling. I miss my boy. I miss him, Charlotte. Why did Fred Duncan have to drive that night? Why did all this happen? I don't think I'll ever know. I do know this; Blake has been able to save ten people's lives so far. The doctor told me that Blake could save up to almost seventy-five people through his tissue donation. I always knew Blake was destined for something great. In his short life, he has saved ten people and counting. That is an amazing thing."

I remained silent. Intently listening for Trish to continue. I could tell she was crying. As tears rolled down my cheeks I prayed silently for her.

I was speechless as I listened to Trish. Tears kept going down my cheeks. I couldn't even fathom how she could have so much strength as she was talking. I knew God was with her. But what she said after this truly blew me away...

"Charlotte, there are a few things I wanted to

say to you. First, I felt it was important to tell you not to feel guilty. I believe with all my heart that God doesn't call us home until it's our time to go home to be with Him. It's like we are all standing in line. We can't get out of the line. We can't switch spots with someone else when it's our time; it's our time. As much as I hate it, and I still don't understand it, it was my sweet boy's time to be with the Lord. It gives me peace knowing that Aaron was there with him in his last moments. He loved Aaron like his own brother. Those two always had fun together. Even though I'm trying to be strong...I know what I believe...I know that Blake is with Jesus...I'm joyful...But I'm angry about all of this too..."

I heard Trish start to weep. I instantly started praying that God would give her strength. My heart was aching because of the pain that Trish was feeling. I just wanted to wrap my arms around her and cry with her.

Trish continued, "I know I'm probably confusing you with my going back and forth on trusting God and being strong...and being angry about losing my sweet boy...but I can't help it, Char. I guess it's true what they say...grief is messy. Yes, I have God's overwhelming peace with me. Yes, I'm angry that Blake had to leave me now. I won't get to watch my sweet boy become a man. I won't get to see him become a husband and father. Yes, I'm hurting...I don't know why it had to be Blake, who passed away, and Fred Duncan is fine. I don't get any of it. But here's what I do know...I know my boy is with Jesus. There's no greater place to be than that. My boy is seeing things that we all long to see. My sweet boy finished strong. He finished strong and spent his last moments on earth with his best friend and brother. My sweet boy has saved lives. Oh, Charlotte, Charlotte, do you think that Aaron would be able to share this with everyone at Blake's funeral? That's another reason why I called about Blake's funeral. I wanted to play that recording you all had of him at church when he was telling his testimony to the youth group. Do you all still have that video?"

"First, please don't apologize about grieving. You're so much stronger than you realize. Grief is messy. You just need to remember that it is a process. I hope you know that you can call me anytime if you need a listening ear. Yes, I believe we do have the testimony video. I'll have my assistant look at the church to make sure and have her e-mail it to me. I will talk to Aaron about sharing. I bet he will. I know he wanted to help in whatever way he could. He loved Blake...he still loves him. Nick and I will always see Blake as our own kiddo. Blake and Aaron have been thick as thieves forever, it seems. I know Aaron is feeling lost without Blake. I also know he feels guilty like it's his fault that Blake is gone. Trish, I hope you know that we are here for you all. If we can do anything for your family, please know that we are more than happy to do anything for you. Blake will always have a special place in our hearts. We miss him terribly. We love you all very much."

"Thank you, Charlotte. Charlotte, you are stronger than you realize. You always are taking everyone's stuff on your shoulders. We are in this together, you know. We've all been through trauma through this sitaution...its changed all of our lives. We will need each other in the upcoming days, weeks, and months. I do not doubt that you all will be there if I need anything. If you can help me get that testimony video, I think that would bless a lot of people. I know that Aaron's testimony about Blake being with Jesus will also be an amazing testimony to bless people. If it's alright, can I come by later today and pick up the video? I'd also like to talk to Aaron if that's alright? If he's not ready, I understand that too, but if he is, I'd love to talk to him."

"I'll talk to Aaron about that, Trish. I know he's going to be flooded with all kinds of emotions. I know he will just give you a big hug and cry. What time do you think you would be coming by?"

"I'll probably come around five or so if that's alright?"

"That's just fine. Also, Nick wanted me to tell you that he and other officers wanted to help escort you all to the burial, if that's alright? We know that Blake was thinking about becoming an officer like Nick. So we wanted to honor him with that."

Trish started to cry... "Oh my, yes, that would be perfect. Thank you all so much. Love you guys. I know Blake loved you all like his own parents too. I know that would mean the world to him."

After we said our goodbyes, I got off the phone. I used all the strength I had to get through that phone call. I looked at Nick and started to weep some more. I pressed my head into his chest and let him wrap his strong arms around me. I felt as though I was melting into his chest. I was trying to stay strong because we had everyone over. But I couldn't help it.

I could tell Nick was wondering what was being said. But he patiently waited. Everyone was still enjoying themselves at breakfast. I could see that Roxy was trying to figure out what was going on. Roxy was waiting patiently and trying to help me out by being the hostess until we got done, which I was extremely grateful for. Roxy is always a rock for me when I need her.

After a few minutes, I noticed that everyone started coming towards us. They all brought their chairs and some sat down on our steps. Roxy took charge and asked Aaron, Erica, and the rest of the kids to go do something for a little bit while the adults talked. I looked at Roxy and quietly whispered, "thank you sis." I was so thankful she stepped in. I didn't want the kids to see me like this. Nick gently wiped the tears from my cheeks. I looked at him and attempted to smile. I gently rubbed his leg. I wanted him to know that I was thankful that he was there with me.

For a few minutes, there weren't any words that were said. We all were just quiet. Then, finally, Violet went into the house to get some more Kleenex for me. When she gently handed Nick the Kleenex box, he pulled out a couple of tissues. He sweetly passed them to me and gently swept the hair away from my face; I lifted my head from his chest and turned to see all our sweet friends just looking at me. They all had sweet expressions on their faces. I could tell they were trying to figure out what was going on. But, of course, I could count on Roxy to break the ice...

"Char, what's going on? We all want to know. We love you, and we are here for you."

Tracey also lovingly chimed in, "What's up, Char? We all love you, and we want you to know that we are here to support you and your family. Are you okay? What can we do for you all?"

I looked at their loving faces and said, "That was Trish. She was talking about Blake's funeral. She wanted to know if I had Blake's testimony from youth. She wants to play that at his funeral. I also told her about what Aaron said..."

Tommy and Julie both looked at me and teared up because they knew what Aaron had said. Everyone else had no idea what I was talking about. I looked around; I saw that Aaron and Erica were on the golf cart, driving down our driveway to drive around a little bit. Which honestly was cute to watch. They both had casts on one leg.

I then proceeded to say to the group, "That was Trish...Blake's mom. I shared with her about what happened...After Aaron woke up from his coma, he proceeded to tell Nick and me what happened that horrible night. He told us how Blake got in the driver's seat. Blake begged Aaron to sit in the driver's seat and drive to the game. Aaron knew that we only wanted him to drive his car, but he went ahead and let Blake drive. Blake was trying to show off in front of Tory because he liked her. Aaron said before he knew it; that's when he saw the headlights coming towards them. That's when everything went dark. Then before he knew what had happened, he saw Blake and Jesus. Blake didn't say anything, but he looked at Aaron and smiled. Blake's attention was focused on Jesus. Jesus told Aaron that he still had stuff for him to do. It wasn't his time yet. Then Aaron woke up to firefighters trying to get him out of the car. That's when everything went dark again. I told Blake's mom Trish about the part where Aaron saw Blake with Jesus. She wanted to know if Aaron would share that testimony a Blake's funeral. She wanted to come by this evening around five. So, in a little while, Nick and I will talk with Aaron to see if he would be interested and able to share."

As I looked around at our sweet friend's faces, there wasn't a dry eye. Everyone was tearing up.

"Wow. That's amazing, Char. Like that honestly

gets me freaking excited! If anyone has any doubts about what happens after we die, this very thing might be the thing that saves them. How powerful is that?" Jordan said.

We all looked at Jordan and smiled. We all sat there without saying anything else. I could tell we all agreed; what if this powerful testimony saves people at the funeral? What if lives change because of this testimony?

Of course, Mark broke the ice by saying something funny, out of the box, and morbid...

"You all know what I want at my funeral? I want Roxy to be wearing something hot. I also want there to be a fiesta! Everyone goes home with tacos or nachos. Also, I want my ashes sprinkled in fireworks, and I want the guys to shoot those suckers high into the sky!"

We all went instantly from crying and reflecting to loud laughter. Then, of course, Roxy hits Mark on the arm.

Roxy said, "My goodness, babe! Where the heck did you come up with all that?"

Mark responded, "You know how I get sometimes? When things get too serious, I've got to joke about something. It's how I function."

"It's okay, Mark; we all love you and your goofy sense of humor," I replied.

I felt like my emotions were everywhere. I was laughing at Mark and tearing up because of my conversation with Trish. After wiping my eyes and blowing my nose, I could feel everyone's eyes staring at me. I looked at Roxy, and without saying anything, she could tell it was time to go ahead and call it a day. So she gave me a hug and whispered, "I love you sis. If you need anything, I'm here for you. Always."

"Alright everyone, let's start cleaning stuff up. I'll get the table clothes. Violet and Taylor, will you all get the leftovers boxed up? Julie and Tracey, would you mind helping me wipe the tables down? I need all the men to help tear down tables and stack the chairs." Roxy announced.

Everyone sweetly started picking up the trash and cleaning up together. Luckily, the kids were all still playing with the animals, and they seemed unbothered by everything. I love the resiliency of children. I long for that same kind of resiliency.

After everything was cleaned up. We all stood around and talked a little while longer.

Aaron and Erica started driving up the driveway and Jordan of course had to joke with both of them about having one cast on each of their legs. Jordan is always good about bringing humor in every situation. He even grabbed Aaron's crutches and attempted to do tricks on the crutches...which then turned intoJordan somehow getting on top of the roof and he jumped into our pool. All the kids thought it was hilarious.

"Well, I think we better head on out. I know you

all need some more rest and to digest everything. We will be praying about your meeting with Trish today. We will also be praying for Aaron. That's a big responsibility. I know he can do it, though." Zach said.

Nick went over and hugged Zach and all the guys.

"Thank you all for coming. Char and I love and appreciate all of you. This meant the world to us. Thank you." Nick replied.

"Yes, thank you all so much. We are grateful to call you family. We will keep you updated on everything. I think we will find out today when Blake's funeral will be. So we will let you know." I added.

After everyone left, Nick and I talked with the kids about Blake's mom coming over. When we started the conversation, Aaron's eyes started getting glossed over. I could tell he was trying not to cry.

"Mom, how am I going to face her? I don't even know what to say. I...I...I mean, like, it should have been me, you know? Like it really should have been me in that seat. If Blake hadn't moved, it would have been me!" Aaron shouted. He then proceeded to go out the front door as quickly as he could on his crutches. Finally, he sat down on the porch swing.

Nick and I looked at each other, and then we looked at Lucy and Landon. Landon seemed pretty upset. Lucy had crocodile tears in her eyes. They both came over and sat down with Nick and me. Nick held Lucy in his lap.

Landon just leaned his head on my shoulder. Nick looked at me, and I nodded at him to say something. I was speechless.

So, Nick looked at Landon and Lucy and said, "It's going to be alright, kids. Aaron has been through a lot. We all have. It's just going to take time to process everything. So, let's just give Aaron some space for a little bit. How about I call Grandma and Grandpa to see if they can take you all to a movie or something?"

"Daddy, we just want to stay here with you all if that's alright," Lucy responded.

After about ten minutes went by, Aaron came back inside. He didn't say anything. He just went upstairs and shut his bedroom door. Landon and Lucy looked at Nick and me. We just smiled

The kids were lying on the couches, covered in soft and cozy blankets. They watched a movie and relaxed. Bowden and Zeus were lying on top of Lucy's blankets. They think they are small pups when they take up most of the couch in reality. I was surprised that Lucy could even be comfortable with these big fur babies lying on her.

As we all were relaxing and taking it easy, we heard Aaron come down the stairs. Slowly but surely, he got to the bottom of the stairs. Landon helped his big brother get to the recliner. I looked at the clock and Trish was coming soon. I went ahead and got Blake's testimony together and put it on a drive so that Trish could have it forever to hold onto. I forewarned the kids that Trish was going to be at our house soon, so that they could all prepare themselves as best as they could.

When we heard the doorbell ring, my heart sank. I prayed and asked God to give me strength. When Nick answered the door and I saw Trish, all I could do was open my arms to hug her. We both started crying. When Trish saw Aaron she held her arms open to hug him.

She looked at Aaron and said, "I want you to listen to me sweetheart...I want you to know, it's not your fault. It's not your fault Aaron. Don't let the enemy torture you with that false idea. God had a plan to take Blake home that night. I know it hurts you. It hurts all of us. But from what I hear, you know without a doubt where Blake is. Isn't that right?"

"Yes mam. I saw Blake with Jesus that night. Blake smiled at me and was so peaceful. He didn't say anything to me, but the look on his face said it all. He was at peace. I just wish I could have helped him. I...I...I can't help but feel like it should have been me. It should have been me. I'm sorry, I'm trying to be strong, but I don't understand. Why did I live? Why did he die? Why did this all happen? I lost my best friend...my best friend. I want my best friend back. I know he's in a better place. I know he's with Jesus."

Aaron began to cry. We all just hugged each other and wept. At that point, no one could say or do anything but cry. Even the dogs tried to comfort us. Sometimes crying cleanses, the soul. It helps heal us. I guess in some ways, this was a needed thing for all of us to have a little closure.

I invited Trish to sit at the dining room table with us. I had my laptop open so that she could watch

Blake's testimony. Before we started watching it, I made sure to grab the sweet tea and tea cookies and sweets that Violet brought over for us. When I sat everything down to help make everything inviting, I saw Aaron start to prepare himself to read his testimony. I quickly but discreetly sat down because I didn't want to miss anything.

"I...I...I'd like to tell you what happened that night if that's okay?" Aaron asked.

"Yes, that's okay with me Aaron. I would love to hear all about it." Trish responded.

"Okay...so...That night was like a normal night you know? Blake and I were excited to go to the varsity game. The girls were going to meet up with us. Blake really liked Tory, which is Erica's best friend. He wanted to impress her. On our way to the game Blake and I were talking about how we hoped Coach would see our dedication and it would help us be on varsity next year. As I said, Blake had this huge crush on Tory and begged me to switch sits with him at this four way stop sign. We were kind of arguing about it because I told him that my parents said no one else could drive my car. He wasn't trying to disobey my parent's rules, he just wanted to impress Tory. I finally went ahead and did what he wanted. Before I knew what happened, I saw headlights coming right at us. I remember Blake shouting, "Jesus!" Then...then that's when I realized we were in trouble. I turned my head away and made eye contact with Erica, and I could see the terror in her eyes. Then that's when everything went dark for a minute. I saw a bright light and Blake and I were with Jesus. Blake smiled at me, and Jesus said, "It's not your time yet Aaron. I've got more for you to do. I'll come get you when it's time." I saw Blake smile so big as he looked at Jesus and then I woke up. I was trapped in the car. That's when I heard the firefighters working on getting me out of the car. That's all I remember. Then I woke up."

We all sat there listening to everything. This was the first time that Landon and Lucy heard the full story of what happened. They both were sitting in awe of what had happened. I looked over at Trish and she just had tears going down her cheeks. I looked at Nick and he was already on his way to get the Kleenex box. Everything was quiet for a few minutes...then Trish said something that I won't ever forget.

"Aaron, thank you for sharing what you experienced with Blake. I want to remind you again, please don't blame yourself kiddo. God knew what was about to happen. It didn't catch God off guard. He knew that Blake was about to go be with Him forever. It's amazing that you got to escort Blake to Heaven. What an amazing gift that is. Aaron, if you're willing, I'd like you to share how you escorted Blake to Heaven at his funeral. I know that I'm asking a lot from you to share about what happened, but I must keep holding onto the hope that God has a good plan. God doesn't waste anything. God always works for the good of those that love Him. We all love the Lord don't we?"

We all agreed. Trish gave Aaron a hug and then we all watched Blake's testimony together. It was last year at church camp. Blake told his testimony of how he came to know the Lord. He talked about how he knew God was real and how when he started to follow the Lord, he had a heart change. He could tell how when God came into his life, he knew he couldn't go back to how he was, he was forever changed.

As we all watched Blake and his sweet testimony, we laughed together. Blake threw some jokes in there, and you could see him look at Aaron in the video to see if he could get Aaron to laugh, which is something he often did. It seemed surreal that Blake wasn't going to get to go to camp with us again. He wasn't going to get to joke with Aaron and call me Momma C. It was almost unbelievable that this was our reality now...

After Blake's testimony was over, we all just sat quietly around our kitchen table. The silence was almost deafening. Trish and I made eye contact and the tears started flowing. Aaron just sank in his chair with his hands on his face. Then we all started crying. It was almost as if the tears wouldn't stop. The loss was magnified in this moment. None of us would get to talk to him again...that is until we go to be with the Lord ourselves. Even though it brings us peace knowing where Blake is and the fact that we will see him again, it still is so hard and heartbreaking.

Lucy softly started to speak...

"Why don't we share a couple of funny stories about Blake? I know Blake wouldn't want us to just cry. He wants us to laugh and smile when we think of him. I'll start...Aaron remember that one time that mom and dad went on a date and left you and Blake to watch us? Blake convinced me that I was invisible...so I went to your room and started throwing toilet paper! I was laughing so loud because I thought I was going to get away with it! But then you all made me pick it up... remember bubba?"

"Oh my gracious! My boy convinced this sweet girl she was invisible? Now, that is funny. You know Lucy, Blake always said you were like his little sister.

He truly loved each of you so much."

"I remember that one day when Blake tried to toilet paper our house and dad made water balloons! We hid out on the side of the house, but we didn't realize that Aaron was in on it too. Then they started spraying us with silly string! Remember that? That was freaking hilarious!" Landon said.

Aaron started to laugh, "That was epic! Oh man, we talked about that for weeks! We talked about it one day at lunch and Blake was drinking a chocolate milk. He laughed so hard that chocolate milk came out of his nose!"

"You all have blessed me so much this evening. Thank you for sharing funny stories and for watching Blake's testimony with me..."

Trish continued, "Aaron, thank you for sharing your testimony about what happened. I can't put into words how much you all mean to me. Thank you for loving my boy so well. I know that he felt like this was his home away from home. He felt safe here. He felt loved."

After Trish left, we all sat in the living room. Even though I was completely exhausted, I knew that everyone loved homemade chocolate chip cookies. So I had Lucy help me make them. She always loves to cook with me. After we enjoyed the cookies, we all went to bed. We were all emotionally drained and mentally exhausted. The next couple of days went by pretty fast. It was amazing to watch Aaron prepare his testimony for the funeral.

The day before the funeral, we asked Aaron what

he wanted to do for the day. We knew that tomorrow was going to be pretty tough on Aaron...on all of us.

Nick and I went to Aaron's room. I looked at Nick to take the lead in the conversation, "So bud, what do you want to do today? We can do anything you'd like to do. We can go for a walk, go watch a movie, go to the mall, play some board games, whatever you want kiddo."

"Honestly, Dad, I just want to have a lazy day. I want to lay around and watch a movie. I honestly might take a nap today too. The past week or so has been a roller coaster ride." Aaron said.

"I get that, son. I definitely get that." Nick responded.

We all decided a nice lazy day was an excellent way to spend the rest of our day. I noticed that shortly after Nick and I went and talked with him, Aaron went outside to sit on the porch swing. I decided to go outside to be with Aaron a little bit. I simply listened to his heart about what had happened. I tried to reassure him that it wasn't his fault, and I just allowed him to vent. After Aaron and I talked for a while, I saw him release some of the stress and guilt he was carrying. It was still there, but he was trying his best to just go through this process of accepting what had happened and not living in a state of mind of "I could have, I would have, or I should have."

"Mom, I'd love to hear Blake's voice again. I know his mom is going to share his testimony and I'll be sharing about what happened that night. Maybe Blake and I together can help save someone through our testimonies. I know what this entire experience has done for my faith. I can only imagine what it will do for someone else's faith. I think I will go to my room and write down what happened. That way, I can make sure I don't leave anything out. Isn't that what you do when pastors preach? They write down their sermon notes so they don't forget?"

I hugged Aaron and said, "Yep, buddy, that's exactly what they do. I'm so proud of you, son. The strength you are showing me and everyone who knows you are inspired. I know God will give you the words you need."

Aaron smiled at me and hugged me. Then, he went inside, and I sat on the swing for a while longer. I was just absorbing everything that Aaron said. In his short years of life, I was thinking about how my son is already so much further and more assertive in his faith than I was at his age. I'm so thankful for that. Then, after a few minutes, I heard the door open and shut. When I turned to see who it was, Nick had two iced teas in his hands.

"Hey there, beautiful. Can I sit by you a second?" He asked.

"Of course you can, babe. I had a sweet conversation with Aaron. He was processing every-thing. This has all happened so fast. All of it. It seemed like an eternity ago; we were just getting ready for fall break. So much has happened in this short amount of time. It's like we've been on the mountain top and the valley all within a short period. It's easy to go into that mindset of waiting for the other shoe to drop. Like something else bad is going to happen. First, it was Mark. Which praise God, he's okay. Then God answered our prayers for Violet when

Will came along. Then all of this with the car accident, losing Blake, Jean, and almost losing Aaron. Tommy and Julie could have lost Erica. Tory's parents could have lost her too. It's just so much, babe. So much. Then here's our son, pouring his heart out to me. Yet, he already gets it. His faith in the Lord is so strong. Stronger than he realizes. Lord knows I'm a hot mess. I don't feel like I've handled any of this to the best of my ability. I'm just feeling like I'm treading water, babe. What's wrong with me? Why can I encourage others, but when it comes to my own faith, I can't...I can't encourage my own faith. Why is that?"

"Char, listen to me. Your faith has kept me going for more than a time or two. Your faith has helped me become a better man. Your faith has helped countless teens and their families. Your faith has helped every single person you come in contact with. Do you know why? It's because your faith, my love, is pure. You are always transparent with your struggles. You never pretend to be someone or something that you're not. You confess that you need the Lord in your life. The way you live your life Char is one that many aspire to live. Babe, I think you are too hard on yourself."

"Nick, I love you. Thank you for always having my back. I just feel heavy-hearted, I guess. I'm just completely exhausted. I'm worn. I'm praying everything goes smoothly with the funeral tomorrow. Trish asked me to do the ceremony when she came over the other night. She thought that's what Blake would have wanted. Am I going to break down or be strong? Am I going to cry and be a hot mess? Will I know what to say and how to say it? I'm just...I'm just worried I won't do the right thing or say the right thing."

"Char, you're going to do just fine, babe. Plus, all

of us are in this together. You're not alone. I got you. We can lean on each other. It's okay, babe."

I looked at Nick and just wrapped my arms around his neck. I kissed him and just didn't want to let go. This man of mine is so good to me. I love and adore him. After our sweet talk, we went inside. The rest of the day was relaxing. We watched a movie with the kids and binged one of our favorite television series. We even ordered in our favorite pizza. It was what we all needed.

It was time for Blake's funeral. As we were all getting ready that morning, I could tell Aaron was anxious. I went to Nick and had him go take Aaron to pick up some donuts for us to eat before we go. I knew that Aaron just needed to get his mind on other things a little bit.

At Blake's funeral, many came to know the Lord. By Aaron's testimony of what happened that night and Blake's testimony at camp, the two of them together helped save several souls that day. Students that I have prayed for, for a long time came to know the Lord that day at Blake's funeral.

After Blake's funeral, we even had news crews want to interview Aaron about what had happened that night. Churches called from all around that heard Aaron's testimony. Radio shows and podcast shows called and wanted Aaron on their shows. It was a lot to think about. But, of course, we told Aaron to wait a little while. We wanted him not to get thrown into something when everything was still fresh and raw.

Chapter Seven

BACK TO SCHOOL

A week went by, and Aaron shared with us that he was officially ready to go back to school. He wanted to get back in a routine. Nick and I both agreed that Aaron was ready. We kept him home for a week just because we honestly wanted to make sure he was okay. So much has happened in a short amount of time.

Honestly, I don't know how Aaron has handled everything with the grace that he has. The only explanation is God. God has helped our sweet boy push through. God has helped all of us get through these dark valleys. God is the one that will continue to guide all of us as we walk through the valleys and mountaintops. Life is messy, but it's also beautiful. I'm so proud of my children and how they all have handled everything. They are so much stronger than they realize.

The kids all came downstairs to eat breakfast. No one was arguing over the bathroom. Everyone was just simply enjoying their morning. Nick went to the kitchen table to eat with us too. I was so thankful that the Chief let him use his two weeks off so that he's able to stay home for a month with the family as we all get back into our routines and find our new normal.

"Well kiddos are you all excited to all go to school today?" Nick asked while sipping his coffee.

"I am! I think we are going to start learning about volcanos in science today! I'm hoping that I can pick my partner. Last time Mrs. Smith made me partner with Cody. Which was fine, but then everyone saying that I liked Cody and it embarrassed me. I mean, Cody is cute and all..."

Nick looked at our sweet Lucy with a puzzled and frazzled face and said, "Wait a minute there...sweet girl are you saying you've got a crush on someone? I'm not ready for that just yet. Remember, you've got two big brothers and a dad that has to meet who you like first. Also, there's that rule we have about not dating till you all are sixteen. There's a reason why mom and I have that rule. It's because when we were younger, we didn't make the best decisions and made some pretty big mistakes because we dated too early. So we just want you all to be better off than we were at your age."

Lucy started laughing, "I know daddy. I can think a guy is cute without dating him right? I just think God did a good job when he made Cody...that's all."

Nick looked over at me in bewildermint. He was in complete shock that his baby girl was saying these things about a boy.

I couldn't help but laugh as I poured myself a cup of coffee. Nick's face looked so cute. He was in shock that his baby girl was entering this stage of thinking boys are cute and wanting to date. These sweet and innocent conversations helped make everything seem... well...normal. Also, hearing my daughter say that God did a good job making Cody was too funny not to laugh. I swear, the things my kids say sometimes are pure gold.

"So, who's going to take us to school this morning?" Landon asked.

Nick and I looked at each other and I could tell he was about to do rock, paper, scissors...so that's exactly what we did. I ran over to him, and it was game on!

"Rock, paper, scissors, shoot! Rock, paper, scissors, shoot! Rock, paper, scissors, shoot! Dead gummit Char, quit picking the same ones I am!" Nick said and laughed loudly.

The kids and I were laughing because we know that Nick is super competitive. Landon even spit out his milk all over the place because of Nick's facial expression. The dogs were going crazy, Aaron was laughing, and Lucy was too!

"Babe, I'm not, you're picking the same ones as me! You're cheating somehow! I freaking know it!" I shouted.

"Okay, the winner of this round gets to take the kids to school...ready? Rock, paper, scissors, shoot! Rock, paper, scissors, shoot! Rock, paper, scissors, shoot! Oh, my stars Char, this has never happened in the history of rock, paper, scissors! So how the heck are we doing this, babe? Like seriously, quit picking rock! You know what? Why don't we all just go together? I think that's what we should do."

I laughed so hard that I had to sit in Nick's lap to catch my breath. The kids were laughing. Landon even had to get his inhaler because we were all laughing so hard! This was one of those memories I would hold onto forever—just us being...well...us.

As we all started winding down and getting everyone's stuff to head out the door, Nick stopped us and said, "Let's pray together as a family."

We all stood next to each other, and Nick and I put our arms around our children and that's when Nick said the most beautiful prayer...

"Dear Lord, Thank you for today. Thank you for our family. Lord I'm blessed to have Charlotte as my bride and these amazing kids that you've given me. I pray that you be with each of them as they go to school today. Give them courage and strength. Remind them Lord that you are always with them. Thank you Lord that you always go before us, behind us, and you're always beside us. Amen."

"Amen. Thank you babe. Alright you crazy children! Let's take my car. That way you all have more room. Unless you all want to take dad's truck?"

"I will answer for everyone and say, no to the truck. Last time we all packed in dad's truck like sardines, Landon stepped all over my new shoes. I mean, he didn't mean to, but still. I've got my crutches and everything." Aaron said in a concerned voice.

I could tell that he was a bit nervous to go to school, so I agreed with Aaron, and everyone got into my SUV. On our way to school, Nick turned on some 90's rap music and started dancing. The kids all started laughing. Aaron even laughed a bit too. Nick rolled down the windows and had his glasses on. It kind of reminded me of when we first started dating. He would always do this to try to make me laugh and impress me.

When we pulled up to the kid's school I could tell that Aaron was getting hit with all kinds of thoughts and feelings. I know he had to have been thinking that he would be going to school without Blake. I know he was also probably wondering if people would be asking him about the accident or what he saw. So many thoughts flooded my mind while watching the kids start to get out of the car.

"I love you all so much. Remember put a smile on your face, put God in your heart and have a happy day today. Let your light shine bright for all to see."

"Thank you mommy dearest! Thank you padre! Love you both." Lucy replied in a British accent, which she did from time to time. That girl is always practicing for her drama class.

"Thanks mom, see you all later. Love you dad." Landon replied.

"Love you both...If I get ummm...If I get a little overwhelmed today, can I call you all to come and get me?" Aaron asked.

"Of course, bud, no problem. If you need us to come and get you, just text us. One of us or both of us will be here in a heartbeat okay bud?" Nick sweetly replied.

Aaron took a deep breath, "Thanks dad. Thank you mom. Love you both."

Landon handed Aaron his crutches and they all went into the school. When they walked in, all eyes were on Aaron. Some teachers walked up and said hello. Erica was waiting for Aaron by his locker. When Aaron was heading towards his locker, he passed by Blake's locker. It was all decorated and had sticky notes from students on it. Aaron couldn't help but stare at it. He was in shock and a bit distraught.

Aaron accidentally ran into Clide McDaniel and dropped one of his crutches. Clide was the school bully. Aaron was caught off guard. Was Clide going to react? Was he going to start a fight with Aaron? But that's not what happened at all.

Clide picked up Aaron's crutch and handed it gently back to him. "Hey Aaron, I'm sorry about Blake man. He was a good dude. I didn't know him too well, but I do know that he was always nice to me. I got to know him a little in algebra. He was always cracking jokes. One time he made me spit out my soda because of a joke he was telling the class."

Aaron smiled, "Thank you Clide. I miss him a lot. He's my...he...he was my best friend you know?"

Clide gently patted Aaron on the shoulder, "Yeah, I get that. I'm sorry Aaron. You know, I went to his funeral. I sat in the very back, mostly because of how people look at me. But when I heard what you said and I heard Blake tell his testimony, it really...you know? It just did something. It's like it changed my perspective on things. I know that I don't even come close to Blake, but Aaron if you need anything man, I'm here."

Aaron stood there in disbelief. Was this conversation actually happening?

"Thank you, Clide; I appreciate it," Aaron replied.

Aaron turned and walked towards his locker. He was looking down, processing what just happened and as he approached his locker, he looked up and Erica was wearing jeans and a beautiful red top with yellow flowers. The smile she had for Aaron was one that many wish they could have.

She kissed him on his cheek and said, "Hey there good lookin! How are you today?"

"Hey, beautiful girl, I'm good. Did you just see that? Like what just happened? I thought Clide was going to beat me up or something. But instead, he greeted me with kind words, and he even helped get my crutch off the ground. He said that he was at Blake's funeral. He said that my words and Blake's words helped shift his perspective. Can you believe that?"

"Wow, that is amazing Aaron. See, God is up to something. I think that Blake's story and your story are going to be used in a big way. I'll be here with you okay? We are in this together." Erica responded.

The rest of the day went smoothly. It was weird

for Aaron to be without Blake, but the peace surrounding Aaron was evident. God was helping Aaron; everyone could see that. After school, Nick picked up the kids so that I could work on some stuff for the church. When they all got home, I heard lots of chatter. I went into the kitchen, and they all had smiles on their faces. Nick came over and kissed me. Then, we all went to the living room and sat down on our favorite couches.

"Did everyone have a good day?" I asked.

"Aaron, you should tell mom what happened today with that Clide kid," Landon said.

"Wait...are you talking about that McDaniel kid? That's the one that tends to bully people right? Oh gosh, what happened?" I asked in a concerned voice.

"Mom, nothing, it was pretty cool. I accidentally ran into Clide because I was staring at Blake's locker. Everyone decorated his locker and wrote him sticky notes. So when I ran into Clide, I was like, "Oh crap." I thought he was going to punch me or something. But that's not what happened at all. Instead, he just helped me pick up my crutch, and he told me if I needed anything, I could reach out to him. He also said how he was at Blake's funeral, and he heard my story and Blake's story. He said it changed his perspective on things. Can you believe that?" Aaron asked.

I hugged Aaron and said, "Wow bub. That really is amazing. Look at how God is already using this for His glory. This is going to be something that God is going to use for a long time I have a feeling. Aaron, I know you may not fully comprehend all of this now, but I think when Jesus said to you that He had more for you to do, I think this is one of the things. This testimony is going to help people for many years to come. I don't know what that looks like, or what it means. But I do know that God is doing something."

"Why me, though, mom? I'm not qualified to be used by God. I can't...I mean, I don't know a lot of stuff. I only know what I've experienced. I try to read the Bible and everything, but I get distracted. So why would God use me? Honestly, Blake was more of the kind of person God could use, mom."

Nick and I looked at each other. Without saying a word, we both understood what we were thinking. We have both felt this way more than a time or two in our lives. The feeling of not being good enough. The feeling that others would be better for God to use.

Nick went and sat by Aaron, "Aaron, listen to me for a minute. Your mom and I can relate to how you're feeling right now. That feeling that you can't be used is a lie. The feeling that Blake was more of the kind or type of person that God could use, is also not true. God can use anyone son. Has God used Blake to do big things? Absolutely! We believe that Blake's story will be one that will help many people for many years to come. God is using you now son. God is using your story to help people. I mean the evidence is right there for you to see. Even Clide is starting to change. Don't you see son? Don't you see what God is doing right now? God is starting something so big that none of us can truly comprehend it all right now. All we've got to do is seek the Lord, and He will make our paths straight."

I sat there in admiration for what my sweet husband just spoke—words of wisdom and truth. I could tell that Aaron was digesting each word that his father said.

"It doesn't make sense though, why would God want to use me? I mess up all the time. I...I...I'm just not good enough...I just don't get it. I'm trying to understand, but I just don't get it."

"Aaron, daddy, and I have been there several times. We've both thought those thoughts of not being good enough. Not being equipped to do what God wanted us to do. But you must remember that God doesn't call only on qualified ones. God qualifies those He calls. He makes a way where there isn't a way. So let's just keep our eyes on Him and lean on each other. God will direct you. God will direct all of us, bud. We've just got to trust His plans."

That evening before dinner, I could tell that Aaron was reflecting on our conversation. Aaron went outside with Landon and Lucy. They all went to go feed the goats and just hang out together. Nick and I sat on our porch swing, and we were just cuddling and watching our kids just be themselves. It was so relaxing to simply just swing and not worry about anything else. The goats were being crazy of course which always makes us laugh. Oreo always tries to hog the food. Bowden and Zeus always go and try to keep them all in line.

My cell phone beeped, and I got a notification on my email. It was the local news station wondering if Aaron would share his story. I showed Nick and we both were just thinking it over.

"Babe, I'm feeling torn. There's a part of me that's like, "How awesome!" Then there's another part of me that's like, "Yikes, I don't know about this.""

What are you thinking?" I asked.

"Well, babe, I'm thinking that we should ask Aaron what he wants to do. Then we back him up on whatever he chooses to do. If he's not ready, I want to respect that and if he wants to share, I also want to respect that." Nick replied.

I smiled at Nick; he always knows what to say. I kissed him on both of his cheeks and on top of his nose, "Okay, that's what we will do then. Let's ask him tonight okay? That way we can know how to answer these emails. If he's ready or wants to share great, and if he's not ready or he doesn't feel led to share then great. Either way is fine. I just want him to do what he feels like God is calling him to do. Maybe he doesn't understand that yet, but I think after our talk, he will know what he needs to do."

After we all ate dinner together, we all were just doing the norm. Everyone was in the living room watching re-runs of our favorite television shows. Lucy was all cuddled up in her favorite fuzzy blanket. Zeus was cuddling with her on the couch. Landon was playing on his cell phone as he was laying on the floor with pillows and Bowden surrounding him. Aaron was laying in the recliner with his leg propped up as he was texting Erica with a big smile on his face. I was doing the dishes and cleaning up the kitchen a little bit. I can't ever really relax until things are cleaned. Nothing drives me crazier than a messy kitchen.

"Oh my gosh! Oh my gosh!" Aaron said loudly.

"What's going on? Are you okay bub?" Nick asked.

"Yeah, I'm okay. I just got a text from Clide. This is weird. He's wanting to know if he could sit with me at lunch tomorrow. He said that he just had questions about God, and he thought I might be able to help answer them." Aaron said in a surprised voice.

"Wow, bro, that's awesome," Landon said.

"Bubba, I think that's cool. Wouldn't it be cool if Clide changed his life because of you and Blake's lives pointing to God? I think that's so cool! Bubba, what if you become a pastor like mom?" Lucy asked.

Aaron looked at me and smiled, "That would be cool. I mean, I want to be a police officer too, but you never know. So I'd be open to that."

I looked at Nick, he could tell I was getting tears in my eyes. So, he went ahead and chimed in, "That's really cool bub, what are you going to say?"

All of us were kind of staring at Aaron to see what he was going to say. All of us were quiet...then there was a comedic part in the background of our favorite television show. We all instantly went from intensely listening for Aaron's reply to laughing hysterically. It's always the same parts of a television show that are hilarious every single time. I loved how God used that as an icebreaker. I mean we all were intense like a few minutes ago, now we are all laughing hysterically.

"I think I'm going to reply, "Sure. Sounds good," then I'll just pray and ask God to guide me with what to say tomorrow. I mean, I don't have all the answers by any stretch, but I have to believe that God will guide me...right mom?" Aaron asked me.

I went and sat on the couch by Nick and said,
"Yep, that's exactly right. I can't tell you how
many times God had given me words to say when I
had zero clue what to say. God is faithful like that. So
don't be afraid to say that you don't know an answer
if you don't. Just be real. Be yourself, Aaron; you'll do
just fine."

"Thanks mom, I'll do that then. Just be myself...
be myself." Aaron said to himself quietly.

After our show was over Lucy and Landon both
decided to go to their rooms. Nick and I asked Aaron
to hang tight and talk with us for a little bit before going to bed.

"Hey bub, mom and I wanted to talk to you
about something...mom has received a few emails from
local news networks wanting to interview you about
your story with what happened that night. They are
wanting to hear about how you went to heaven and I'm
sure they are also going to interview you and ask you
what happened with the car accident as well. As far as
the accident goes, I wouldn't really say anything about
what happened with Fred Duncan, especially because
of it being an opened case and the trial will be coming up soon. But if you're wanting to talk about what
happened with you escorting Blake to heaven and what
that was like, you can. It's up to you. Mom and I support whatever you'd like to do buddy."

I could tell Aaron was thinking about what Nick
was saying. He looked like he was about to say something, but he paused. He was really thinking hard about
this.

"Bub, we want you to know that we really do

113

support you in whatever you choose. We love you very much and we are so proud of you Aaron." I said.

"Mom and dad, I'm humbled by the offer...but honestly, I don't have a desire to share that on a news platform. I was thinking about what dad said with Fred Duncan and the trial. I know that will be broadcasted on every local news station. So, I'll have to pray a lot and gear up for that. I'm sure they will put up pictures from the wreck and video of the wreckage. I just don't want to deal with that, you know.

"Son, you are wise beyond your years, you know that?" Nick asked.

"I agree with dad on that one. You are so wise for your age buddy."

"It's because I have wise parents. Thank you both for always loving me and supporting me. I always know I can count on you both to be there for me and love me. I've been thinking about that a lot since everything happened. You all didn't leave my side. You didn't condemn me after it happened. You simply loved me, and you all were there for me. I love you mom; I love you pop."

Nick and I both had tears going down our cheeks. We were both amazed at how our sweet boy had so much wisdom. He was making a good choice. He was doing what he felt he was supposed to do. He wasn't chasing fame for his experience; he was chasing after what he felt God wanted him to do. That, to me, was highly admirable.

After we hugged Aaron goodnight, Nick and I cuddled on the couch for a while. I put my head on his chest, and he gently caressed my hair and tickled my back. I think we both were just taking in everything. Nick and I can say so much without saying anything at all. I was listening to his heartbeat and each breath he took. We had nothing to do; all our babies were in bed. The animals were all taken care of; it was just quiet. It's moments like these that I'm grateful for. Just simply relaxing without concern or worry. Just being still, which is something that I struggle with daily. I'm constantly worrying, always doing something, but I rarely remember the importance of simply being still.

I lifted my head up and looked at Nick, "Babe, how did we get so lucky? I mean the wisdom that Aaron has is absolutely amazing."

Nick kissed me softly on my forehead and brushed the hair away from my face, "Honestly sweet-heart, I think he gets a lot of that wisdom from you. I know you always say that he's a lot like me, but I think he's a lot like you too. You know what really got me today? That conversation with Lucy this morning. How is it that our baby girl is talking about how God did a good job making that Cody kid. Which, by the way, I need to see exactly who she's talking about. I'm also going to tell Aaron and Landon to check out this kid."

"Well babe, you know our kiddos are growing up. It won't be long and I'm sure Landon will get a girlfriend. Lucy is getting older like her brothers. I know it's hard because it's your baby girl. You'll still be number one in her eyes babe. She has always been a daddy's girl and I know she always will be."

Nick laughed, "Char, you know she's crazy about you too. But I get what you mean. I love you so much. You ready for bed?"

"Yes, I'm very ready Mr. Johnson. But I could use some lovin first..."

"Now that Mrs. Johnson, I can handle."

Nick picked me up and carried me to our bedroom. We both forgot that Lucy had been doing her dog training for Bowden and Zeus earlier. She was trying to train them to pick up their toys. Nick accidentally stepped on a dog toy that Lucy left out for Zeus. We both started laughing uncontrollably because it was unusually loud.

"Okay Char, you ready to try this again?"

I kissed Nick and replied, "Absolutely Mr. Johnson!"

Then we spent the rest of the night loving on each other and sleeping peacefully in each other's arms. It was what we both needed. We needed each other.

Chapter Eight

AARON'S STORY, MAYOR TRACEY & THE FIRE

The next morning while making the kids breakfast, I received a text message from Tracey. She told me how she wanted to have a campaign party and was thinking about having it at the FOP, which is the Fraternal Order of Police. They have an event room where they have their police and police family conferences. The Chief gave her the go-ahead, so that's what she's going to do. She wanted to know if the girls and I would like to get together and help her set everything up. So, I, of course, said, "Yes! Absolutely!"

Nick walked into the kitchen, and I danced as I walked towards him, "Hey babe, guess what? Tracey just sent me a text message about her campaign party. We are going to have it at the FOP and the girls, and I are going to help her put it together. Doesn't that sound like a blast?"

"Anything with Tracey and Keith is a blast. So yes, that sounds awesome! So when is she going to be doing this?" Nick asked.

"She's going to keep me updated, but I'm guessing in the next week or two," I replied.

The kids all came down the stairs to eat. Lucy came down last, because she was practicing curling her hair with the curling wand, which takes her a little longer than usual.

"Mom, Lucy was taking forever in the bathroom this morning, can you please tell her that she needs to kick it up a notch or two?" Landon asked in a frustrated tone.

Nick tried not to smile, "Okay, Lucy babe you do need to either wake up a little earlier or something so that your brothers can do whatever they need to do to get ready, okay?"

"Okay Padre. I'll try to wake up earlier, but today only took me longer to get ready because of that stinkin curling wand, which I burnt my wrist on this morning." Lucy answered.

"You burned yourself? Let me see." Nick replied.

As Lucy turned over her wrist to show him, there was a little burn mark on her wrist. Nick gently picked up her arm and kissed her wrist. Lucy looked at her daddy and smiled. She's always been a daddy's girl.
Aaron was kind of quiet as he was eating his

scrambled eggs and cinnamon toast. I could tell he was in deep thought about his day. I figured he was going over in his mind what he was going to say to Clide today.

"You doing okay bub?" I asked.

"Yeah, just thinking about everything, you know?" Aaron replied.

I hugged Aaron, "Yeah, I get it kiddo. It's all going to be alright. I know God is guiding you. Just take a deep breath and know that God always goes before you, He's beside you, and behind you. There's nowhere that you go, where He isn't there. That's the beautiful thing about God. He meets us where we are. God will give you the words you need to encourage Clide."

"Thank you mom." Aaron softly replied.

After taking the kids to school, Nick and I decided to go have a date day. This is something that we would do often when he worked the night shift. We decided to go see a movie and go to lunch at our favorite place, "The Chicken and Waffle Shack." We both needed this so much after the hectic time we had the past few weeks.

We always love going to "The Chicken and Waffle Shack." The atmosphere is the best part. It's a huge barn with lights hanging everywhere inside and multiple picnic tables outside. They have pickleball courts and cornhole. It's just a fun and unique restaurant. We also love that it's locally owned. I always love looking up at all the great lights they have strung up inside. There is always live music, and they have a bar too.

Nick and I love to dance together. Dancing together is something we've done since we started dating. It doesn't matter what kind of music is being played, that's what we always do when coming here. We aren't afraid to bust out our unique dance moves. Even if no one else is, we don't care. As far as we are concerned, it's just him and I. That's all that matters when we are on the dance floor.

Nick gave me an ornery side-eye and said, "Hey babe, watch this..."

Then before I knew what happened, Nick started doing the robot and he started doing the fish dance! I was laughing so hard; I almost peed my pants. I feel like we have been walking through such tough times the past few weeks and this was something we desperately needed.

As I laughed and admired my goofy husband making these bizarre dance moves, I felt my cell phone vibrate. I knew it was a text, so I looked to see what it was, and it was a text from Aaron. It said, "Mom, I just talked to Clide, and it went better than I thought. I can't wait to tell you all about it when I get home!" I would tell Nick about it, but as I watched him flopping around on the floor with a huge smile, I had to watch this play out. I couldn't interrupt him...I mean...I guess I could, but I don't want to.

I even recorded a video on my phone and sent it to Keith, Zac, Mark, and Jordan.

They all instantly laughed, and Keith said, "Are y'all at the Chicken and Waffle Shack?"

"Yes we are and your boy over here is acting all

kinds of goofy!" I quickly replied.

"Okay, don't tell him but we aren't too far away from there. We just left a call; Zac and I will come by really quick and see what that fool is up to." Keith replied.

I gave them the go-ahead, and I kept smiling big at Nick. I could tell he was trying to figure out what I was up to, but he had no idea that Zac and Keith were about to sneak up on him. About five minutes went by, and suddenly, I saw Keith come through one door and Zac through the other door. I was trying to keep a straight face because Nick's back was facing them.

"Well...well...well...what kind of situation do we have here?" Keith said in a goofy voice.

Nick quickly turned and saw Keith and Zac standing there, holding their belts.

"Its my boys!" Nick shouted with excitement.

Keith and Zac sat down at our table and talked with us for a few minutes. I love watching Nick's face light up when he sees the guys and how they act with each other. They have a brotherhood and closeness together. It does my heart good to see them all together.

"So, what have you all been up to today?" Nick asked.

"Oh, you know, we had one attempted robbery, some traffic stops, an attempted suicide, a stolen car, and we had a prostitute going around to a few of those hotels up on NW 10th street trying to get business.

But instead, she's had multiple complaints called about her." Zac replied.

"Wow, the things you all see day today. It's a lot. Every time Nick comes home and tells me about his night or day, I am always amazed with everything you all handle. I'm proud of you all and your hearts for our community." I responded.

"Thanks Char. We appreciate everything you all as spouses do too. We know it's not easy having your husband go and do what he does sometimes, but you handle it very well. I'm always amazed with how Tracey handles things too. She's my rock that's for sure. Can you believe that she's running for Mayor? I'm so proud of her. She's really wanting to make a difference in our city." Keith said.

"I know it! I'm so proud of her too. She asked me this morning if the girls and I would help her with her campaign party at the FOP. So, of course, I accepted! I can't wait!"

"That will be a trip for sure! All of you girls together I know equals pure orneriness. Especially you and Tracey." Keith said.

After we visited for a little bit, the guys had to leave to go on another call. They told Nick that they were excited for him to come back in a couple of weeks. I think he was getting excited to go back too. Nick and I enjoyed the rest of our afternoon together. We even played some pickleball after we ate our chicken and waffles.

On our drive to go pick up the kids from school, I was just looking at Nick as he was driving. I was just admiring my sweet husband. I was playing with his hair and tickling the back of his neck. He looked at me and just smiled sweetly and then he looked at me and did that cute eyebrow trick that he does when he raises one eyebrow and lowers the other one. I could tell that this is something we both needed so much. It was a time of just enjoying each other and simply having fun together.

"I wonder how Aaron's talk with Clide went. I can't wait to hear!" Nick said as we pulled into the school parking lot.

It was cute seeing all the kids stand together and wait for us. It was almost like when they were younger, and they were standing in the car line at school. Except back then they were all a lot shorter, and they looked more excited to see us. Teenagers crack me up. They act like they don't care if we are there, but they really love that we are there for them.

Nick and I greeted them and asked them about their days as they all got in the car. Of course, we got some of the typical answers teenagers give their parents and one surprising comment from Lucy.

"My day was good," Landon said.

"My day was good too. I got to see Cody, so all is well in my world," Lucy said as she winked at me.

"My day was pretty cool. But, first, I want to tell you all about what happened with Clide today!" Aaron said with excitement.

"Okay bub, what happened? Daddy and I can't wait to hear."

"Well, it started at lunch. Clide came and sat with Erica and me. He asked if he could just talk to me privately. Erica didn't mind, she went and sat with Tory and Michelle. As Clide started talking to me, he completely opened up about his life. His dad left him when he was seven years old. His mom has been with one abusive boyfriend after another. She just married a good guy that goes to church and everything. Clide hasn't known what to do with this guy that his mom married, because of all the hurt he's had with her past boyfriends. One boyfriend used to hurt his mom and even hit Clide more than a time or two. He's been more open to the idea of God because of his mom's new husband Todd. Which, by the way, I think his step-dad is that Todd guy that came to play at the church's men's basketball team a few months back. Remember that dad? You let Landon, Blake, and I go with you. Anyways, after he went to Blake's funeral and heard my testimony and Blake's testimony, he said God started tugging on his heart. It was unlike anything Clide had ever felt before. The night before I went back to school, he prayed, and he asked God if he was real, to give him a sign. That next day at school, I ran into him. He said that's when he knew. He knew God was real because God used the person who got his attention to run into him. Isn't that amazing?"

"Wow bub! That is amazing! Did he ask you any questions? What did you say? Tell us everything!" I couldn't contain my excitement.

"Honestly, he didn't ask me anything. He just shared his heart with me, and I simply listened." Aaron responded.

"You know son, that's sometimes the most powerful thing. To simply listen is something that a lot of people struggle with. They struggle with listening

124

and think about what they are going to say while the other person is talking rather than listening to simply listen." Nick said.

As we continued to talk and drove closer to home, we noticed that there was smoke the closer we got to our house. In my gut, I had a horrible feeling something was wrong. When we went down our street there were firefighters that were over at Anne and Sean's house. Their house had caught fire. We saw them standing across the street watching in shock as their home burnt down to ash. My stomach sank.

"Oh my gosh, Nick," I said as I turned and grabbed his leg.

"Momma how did that happen? Oh, my good-ness. Why did that happen?" Lucy asked with concern.

"Nick, drop me off by them and then take the kids home. Kids, you all go home and let the dogs out. Take care of the critters. Daddy and I are going to be with Anne and Sean for a while. We will probably ask them if they want to stay the night at our house too. So please pick up everything and make sure the house is clean. Also make sure there are clean pillows and blankets that they can use for the evening. Can you all do that for me?" I asked.

"Yes mam, we will. I'll make sure of it." Landon said responsibly.

When Nick dropped me off, I immediately ran over to Anne and Sean. Anne was in a puddle of tears and Sean stood there with pain and frustration. He had tears coming down his cheeks. I didn't say anything.

I just put my arms around them both as we stared at their house ablaze.

"I...I...I...don't know how this happened. We were just watching television and all the sudden we smelled smoke. Before we knew what happened the house was full of smoke. As we went outside, the roof was on fire, and everything just caught fire so fast. Char, we've lost everything. I don't know how we will be able to recover anything. I...I...I don't know, I just don't know." Anne said in shock.

Sean was just still so silent. I could tell he wanted to fix it and he didn't know how. There wasn't anything he could do except pray and watch as the firefighters tried to put the fire out. A few minutes later Nick pulled up with his truck. He immediately ran over to the firefighters and there were a couple that were guarding traffic. He asked them what they thought happened and because they knew that Nick was an officer, they were able to talk about it a little bit. Nick found out that the fire started in the attic. They think that an animal such as a squirrel got into the attack and possibly chewed up some wiring that caused the blaze to start. They are still looking into it, but that's what it's looking like to them.

When Nick came over to us he said, "I talked with one of my buddies Jimmy. He said that they think that the fire started in the attic. It is looking like a critter like a squirrel, or something got into the attic and chewed some wiring, they are still trying to figure it all out, but that's what it's looking like. I'm so sorry. There are no words at a time like this. Char and I want you both to know that you are more than welcome to stay with us tonight and as many nights as you need."

Sean could not say a word. All he could do was

hug Nick. Nick and I stayed right by their side as we watched the fire die down. When everything was clear, the firefighters gave them the go-ahead to go and look to see if they could salvage anything. Then it started to rain.

In my mind I was thinking, "Really God? Their house just burned down and now you're making it rain?"

Nick and I looked at each other and we both knew that we just had to help them grab anything and everything that we could. So, we all dug through the ash and mud to find scraps of what was left of their keepsakes and treasures. I called Mark, Roxy, Violet, Will, Taylor, Zach, Julie, and Tommy and asked them to help in any way that they could. I told them that we needed to start collecting funds for them and anything we could to help them out during this heartbreaking time. Before we knew what happened, there was several people from our church helping by getting trucks, buckets, gift cards, and just helping any way they could to help salvage any belongings they had left. The community came together in such a big way.

Anne and Sean stayed with us for two days. Those two days were filled with tears and laughter. We hated that they were going through what they were going through, but we loved having them stay with us. It grew us all much closer too. The church came together and paid for a hotel for Anne and Sean to stay at for a month, which was a huge blessing. We even did several fundraisers for Anne and Sean. We were able to raise $200,000 within a week. God took another challenging situation and created beauty literally from the ashes.

Anne had a great sense of humor about everything. She made jokes about how she didn't like her kitchen anyways. She said that she would make her kitchen extra this time around. It truly is amazing when all hell breaks loose in someone's life. That's when their faith is brought to light. You get to see where they place their trust. By watching Anne and Sean process all of this and literally pick up the pieces of their lives, they both displayed complete faith in God. It didn't mean that it wasn't painful, it just meant that they knew that they weren't alone. And that is something beautiful.

Chapter Nine

FRED DUNCAN

A couple of weeks passed, and honestly it felt like a whirl-wind of emotions. Watching our dear friends lose a lot of their possessions, yet they kept their faith and sense of humor. Going through everything we've been through with Aaron and Blake passing away has been exhausting. Watching our dear friend Mark get shot and recover quick-ly by the grace of God.

It just seems like we've been going through valley after valley, with glimpses of mountain tops. The mountain tops are the high places we get to experience in life. The places when we get to love on those that love us. The places where we get to spend time with loved ones. When our loved ones are still with us despite the hardships, most of all, the mountaintops worth holding onto are the ones that inspire us to keep going, to keep the faith.

Little did I know, our family would be walking through another valley. The morning started like any other morning. The kids were eating breakfast. Nick was finally going back to work after taking off for a month. Everyone was getting into their regular routines. I know Nick was excited to get back in uniform and walk in his calling of helping serve and protect those in our community. I was drinking my coffee and moving slowly. For some reason, this morning, I was not awake at all.

I didn't sleep well the night before. I guess I didn't sleep well because I was restless and felt like something was about to happen, and I couldn't figure out what it was...that afternoon, I would find out. After hugging and kissing Nick goodbye and dropping the kids off at school, I had something I hadn't had in a while...alone time. I decided I'd go to one of my favorite boutique stores and grab a coffee at Violet's on the way. I stopped by Violet's and of course sweet Vi had my latte and muffin in hand when I walked in.

"Vi, how did you have that ready so fast? How did you even know?"

Violet smiled at me and said, "Well sweet friend, I saw you in the car. I could tell you were praying or something before you came inside. I figured I'd have your usual ready for you."

I hugged Violet and let out a big sigh of relief. "Thank you Vi. I appreciate you so much sister."

"You're very welcome. What are you going to do today Char?"

"Well, I figured I'd go to my favorite boutique down the street and then I'd just head home and maybe soak in the bathtub and then sit on the porch swing and read a book."

"That sounds amazing Char! Go for it sister! You deserve some relaxation. Oh, by the way, Will and I are doing amazing thanks to you and Roxy! Char, we have even talked about marriage. It all seems like it's so fast, but I guess when you know...you just know."

"Vi! Oh, my stars! I'm so excited! Seriously! Does Roxy know? Do the girls know that this kind of talk is coming out of your mouth right now?"

"Not yet, I thought maybe we could get the girls together sometime soon to talk about wedding plans and stuff."

"Vi! Wedding plans! Okay, I am just a ball full of excitement at this point! Your wedding is going to be freaking amazing okay? I just want you to know, we will all put our heads together and blow your mind! Also, did you talk with Tracey about her campaign party at the FOP yet?"

"Yes, she told me about the campaign party. She asked me to cater to it, which I'm excited about, especially at a major event like that. And I know, my sweet friend, that you girls will be right by my side with the wedding planning. So thankful to have my sisters by my side. Love you, Char."

"I love you too, Vi. Okay, before I start crying happy tears, I'm going to go. Unfortunately, I don't have waterproof mascara on. But I will call you later this evening, okay? Love you, sis."

"Okay, sounds good. Love you too Char. Have a great day sweet friend."

After leaving Violet's and getting in my car, I couldn't help but thank the Lord for that answered prayer again. Violet has been praying and waiting for what seems to be so long to find someone to love and spend her life with.

"God, thank you for being faithful. So much has happened lately, and I feel like I've been treading water, trying to stay afloat. But you always know when I need those little reminders of the prayers you have answered. I'm thankful for all the yeses, the no's, and the wait...not yet's."

When I started to drive away, I turned on my music, sipped my amazing latte that Vi made, and my chocolate chip muffin. I went into the boutique and found a couple of cute shirts for Lucy and a hat, jeans, and a cute shirt for me. When I got to my car and loaded up all my new finds that I was excited about, I started my car. That's when I saw him.

I saw Fred Duncan. He was with his cousin Jay. I sat there, almost paralyzed. I was in complete shock. Thousands of thoughts flooded my mind. I was angry. I was heartbroken. I was, well...pissed. My first instinct was to get out of the car and yell at him. I wanted to punch him in the face. I honestly wanted to cuss him out and tell him that he ruined people's lives because of his selfish choices. As I sat there shaking and fighting against what I really wanted to do, I called Nick.

Nick didn't answer the phone. I went into a panic. I called Roxy, and she didn't answer either. Then I called Violet, and as she answered the phone, I whispered, "Vi, help me, please."

Violet said, "Char? Char? Where are you? What's wrong?"

"Vi, listen to me. Fre...Fred Duncan is outside of the boutique. How is he here? Why the hell is he here, Vi? I can't move."

"Okay, Char, I'm going to come. I'll just have Caranda watch the restaurant. I'll be right there. Did you call Nick?"

"Yes, I called him; he's just not answering. I called Roxy too, but she didn't answer. I hate to bother you when you're at work. But I just didn't know what to do."

"Okay, don't worry. I'm on my way. I'll try to get a hold of someone. Where are you? In your car?"

"Yes, I'm in my car. I put my seat back because I didn't want that drunk bastard to see me."

"Oh...Okay, Char, I'm on my way."

When I was waiting for Violet to come, I finally got a text from Nick. He was on a call and couldn't answer. He asked if I was okay. Of course, I let my emotional mess-self-tell him that I clearly wasn't okay and told him who I saw. All I saw on his text for the next few minutes were dots.................which drives me crazy.

Nick replied, "Oh, Char. I'm so sorry. I heard that he was out on bail this morning. I thought he would just go home and not show his face around town; I guess I was wrong. I didn't want to upset you. Especially because I knew you didn't sleep well last night. I'm sorry, babe, is anyone with you? I don't want you to be alone right now with all that."

"Vi is on her way; I just want to go punch him. I won't, of course, but I want to. I also would be lying if I didn't think about cussing him out. I want to do that too, but I won't. I just want to go home more than anything, babe. I want to take a bubble bath and chill out."

I began to weep. All the emotions that I've had building up from everything, came out in this moment. I was so embarassed...but even more so...I was pissed off.

Nick responded, "Good, I'm glad that Violet is coming to be with you. I'm sorry, babe. Gosh, I'm just so sorry, Char, that this happened. As soon as I get off this call, I'll head to the house to check on you, okay?"

When Violet came, I felt such relief. I knew that I had someone there to support me. I just felt so drained. It was like I ran a marathon, but all I did was stare at someone I didn't like very much. I mean, he almost killed my son, and he did kill Jean and Blake. It's unfair that he's out walking around right now, and Blake and Jean are in caskets, in the ground. It's incredible what anxiety and all these emotions I was feeling were doing to me. Violet ended up driving me home, and she had Will pick her up from my house to bring her back to work after getting me settled at home. On the drive home, I was reticent. However, my mind was going a million miles a minute. I could tell Violet was looking at me, figuring out what words to comfort me.

I was thankful that Vi was able to be with me. She always has a calming way about her. Even though she didn't know what words to say to fix it all, her just being there for me was more than enough. It's what I needed the most at that moment.

It wasn't long after Violet left that Nick drove up into our driveway. I was in the bathtub when he came. When Nick went into the house, he shouted, "Babe, I'm home."

"I'm in here, Nick. I'm taking a bath."

It was so sweet watching him walk into our bedroom. He had a beautiful vase with pink roses in his hand. He was all dressed in his uniform. He took off his belt and came into our bathroom. He brought the flowers in and put them gently on the windowsill so I could enjoy the roses while taking a bath. He put a towel on the ground and just sat by the bathtub.

"Hey, good lookin." He sweetly said as he reached out to hold my hand.

"Hey babe..."

"Are you okay, Char? I'm so sorry this happened. I didn't say anything about him getting out on bail this morning because I wanted you to have a good day. I knew you were going to have a self-care day, which you deserve, but I didn't think this would happen. Honestly, I don't know how he can walk around town and show his face. He literally just killed two people. It makes me so damn mad, Char."

"I know, babe. I know you were just trying to protect me; that's what you always do. You protect me. I'm thankful for that. When I saw Fred, I just froze. I had so much anger towards him. I wanted to punch him; I wanted to cuss him out...I just wanted him back in jail where he belongs. That way, he can't hurt anyone else. Then I thought, what if Aaron was with me? What would he have done? How would he feel to see him? Then I had another thought...he will have to see him when the trial starts. I don't know how to protect Aaron from that. I don't know what to do, babe...what can we do?"

Nick took a deep breath, and then he said, "Honestly, babe, we can't do anything. This is something that Aaron is going to have to walk through. We all are. What we've got to do is keep our eyes on the Lord. We've got to reaffirm to Aaron that we are all in this thing together. There's no way around it. I hate that we will go through it, but we have no other choice. When the kids get home today, just try to hang out and enjoy being with them...then tonight, at dinner, we will talk about what happened as a family. I think transparency with the kids is the only way that we will be able to heal from all this."

As I was listening to Nick, I knew he was right. I just hated that we had to go through all this. But knowing that my sweet husband was here by my side... in his uniform, sitting by the bathtub...trying to comfort me and meet me where I was, was truly one of those mountain top moments. I am so blessed to have a husband who loves our children and me fiercely.

"I think that's a good plan, babe. Thank you for driving home to just be with me. I love the roses, too; that was so sweet. I really appreciate you so much." I said as I held out my soapy hand to hold his.

He looked at me, smiled, and started blowing the bubbles off my hand. I couldn't help but snicker at how he always tried to do something to make me laugh. Then he kissed my hand gently.

"I love you, Char. I always have, I always will. I don't know how, but I know God will not waste any of this. God can take the worst of situations and make them turn into good. This is one of those testing seasons where we must remember that our faith isn't built on the sand where it will quickly fall. We have built our faith on solid ground. Regardless of what happens in this world, we won't be shaken. We have God, and we have each other."

As Nick got up from the cold tile, he dusted his pants and leaned in to kiss me. As I was sitting in the bath, watching him dust off his pants and put his work belt back on, I couldn't help but smile. I just love him so much. After we kissed and said our goodbyes, he left to head back to work. I stayed in the bathtub a while longer. I don't know what it is about my bath time, but it's so relaxing. I heard the dogs barking, so I got out of the bath and put my robe on.

I went towards the front door and saw Roxy's car parked out front. When I opened the door, Roxy held our lunch from one of our favorite Mexican restaurants.

"Hey Char, Nick called Mark and told him what happened, so here I am! I'm sorry I missed your call this morning. I had to take Zoe to the orthodontist this morning. But when I saw I missed your call and Mark got a hold of me and told me what happened, I knew I had to go to our favorite place and bring you some lunch. I'm so very sorry that happened, sis."

"It's totally fine. I'll be alright; it was just a shock...you know what I mean? But Violet quickly came and helped me get home. Nick came by and talked to me and brought me flowers, and now you're here. I'm thankful for my tribe, that's for sure."

Even though I had this day planned out to be a self-care day and have time to just be alone for a little bit, I'm thankful that God put these amazing people in my life to help me when I'm at my worst. Roxy and I spent the rest of the afternoon together, talking and laughing. We planned some stuff for Tracey's campaign party and spoke about Violet's soon-to-be wedding. It was just a fun and sweet time together.

After picking the kids up from school, I told the kids we would go to the gas station to get slushies. This was something we did a lot when they were younger. I guess I wanted to just be nostalgic for the rest of the day. I even ordered pizza for dinner. I knew that would make Nick happy too.

That evening Nick and I talked with the kids at dinner about what had happened that day. They all took it the way I expected. Lucy looked at me with compassion and shed a tear or two. Landon just looked pissed. Aaron was thinking about what had happened. It was almost as if he realized that he would have to face Fred.

After the kids went to bed and all the animals were settled and taken care of, Nick and I went to bed. When we said goodnight, I tried so hard to sleep...but I couldn't. So, I got up and tried to make some tea. I heard someone coming down the stairs. It was Landon. "Hey, mom."

"Hey bud, what are you doing up?"

"I couldn't sleep. Can I have some tea too?"

"Sure, kiddo."

Landon and I stayed up together for about thirty minutes drinking our tea and playing tic tac toe. We didn't talk much because we tried to be quiet and not wake anyone. So, Landon and I attempted to do a sign language that we made up and whispered. This was another mountain top moment that I will cherish forever. These sweet memories of nothing major, just simply enjoying being together.

I think Landon just needed that extra reassurance to ease his troubled mind at the thought of Fred Duncan walking free now. I needed this sweet time with Landon too. It was good for both of us. Finally, after playing twenty tic-tac-toe games and finishing our teas, we both said goodnight in our made-up sign language and went to sleep.

Chapter Ten

THE TRIAL BEGINS

When we woke up the following day, I got a notification on my cell phone. Taylor texted me and said that I needed to brace myself and the kids because the news was starting to report the accident. They were talking about Fred Duncan's trial that would be starting next week.

I sat up in bed and said, "Wow."

"What, babe?" Nick asked as he was in the bathroom brushing his teeth.

"Look what Taylor texted me this morning. Nick, I just don't...I don't know if I can do all this. It's overwhelming."

"Okay, babe, listen to me. We've got to remember that God is in control. No matter what happens. Remember, we talked about the importance of being transparent with the kids. We can do this. We've just got to keep our eyes on the Lord and lean against each other."

"I know what you're saying is right, but there's a part of me that feels like someone opened a puzzle and threw up the puzzle pieces in the air, scattered everywhere. Some pieces are missing, and the puzzle won't go together because of it. That's what I feel like right now. I just don't know how to make sense of all this. Nick, I'm mad. I mean, there shouldn't even be a trial. He's guilty, period! So why do we have to go through this? Why should Trish have to relive this? Why should Jean's family relive this? It's so aggravating."

Nick finished brushing his teeth, gargled his mouthwash, and dried his mouth off. Then he came into the bedroom and sat on the bed.

"Char, we are going to get through this. We will. It's going to suck. It's going to hurt. But it's okay that we are going through the motions of it all. That's normal. Just keep remembering what we've talked about repeatedly; God is with us. We have our faith, and we have each other."

I took a deep breath, "You're right...okay...we can do this. We can get through this together."

We talked with the kids and told them about what Taylor had said at breakfast. They all had peace that surrounded them. It was almost as if God prepared their hearts for this news this morning.

Aaron looked at his siblings, father, and me and said something profound, "You know, I thought about this last night. I felt in my heart that this was going to come about soon. As I sat in my room thinking about all this, I wondered what Blake would do if he were in my shoes. Of course, I know Blake would have righteous anger about what happened, which we all do. But I think Blake would somehow find it in his heart to forgive Fred for what he did. Not because Fred deserves it, but because of the grace God shows us every day. It's taken me a little while to process everything since it happened, but I think that whatever happens, God will use all of it somehow...someway. I'm ready. I'm ready for this. I know you all will be with me. I know Erica and people at school and church will be there too. I don't know why, but I feel like I need to tell Fred that I forgive him. So, when the opportunity arises, that's what I've decided I'm going to say to him."

We all sat in awe of Aaron's strength and faith, which was on full display for his family to see. This impressive sixteen, almost seventeen-year-old young man is convicting this momma's heart of her own thoughts towards Fred Duncan. My reaction was to cuss him out and punch him. I wanted Fred to suffer. But instead, my son's response was to show grace. It stopped me in my tracks. My son taught me a lesson that morning. I had a fit of righteous anger that wanted Fred Duncan to get what he deserved. Still, my son wanted to do the opposite...he wished to give forgiveness and grace to someone who didn't deserve it.

That's when God spoke to my heart. None of us deserve the grace and forgiveness that He gives us daily. But He does it anyway. So if God does that for us and we are supposed to model what God did for us to others, shouldn't we do the same?

I had to excuse myself to my room for a minute. I began to weep. My heart broke. I knew my thoughts and actions towards Fred weren't right. I wanted Fred to go through the worst of punishments. I wanted him to go through hell like we have had to go through for the past month and a half. I wanted him to suffer. I'm a pastor and have these feelings that don't honor the Lord. And then you have my son, who just wants to show compassion and forgiveness. I felt broken at this moment.

Before I knew it, Nick walked into our bedroom.

He saw me crying.
        I didn't have to say anything.
                He knew why I was crying.

"Char, it's alright. It's going to be alright."

After getting my composure back, I washed my face and went back into the kitchen.

"Are you okay, mom?" Aaron asked.

"Yeah, bub, I'm alright. Honestly, you just convicted your momma's heart. You see, kids, I have a lot of anger towards Fred Duncan. I'm pissed at him. I hate the pain he has caused so many people by his negligence. He killed Jean and Blake. He almost killed Aaron, Erica, and Tory...yet he's walking free right now. I guess you could say when you started talking, Aaron...God convicted my heart. My attitude has been so hateful. I had no grace in my heart towards him...all I had was hate. I had to excuse myself because I needed God to help me with the anger and hate that I have in my heart towards Fred."

The kids were all digesting what I was saying. I could tell that they were surprised to hear me say that I had hate in my heart towards Fred, but I could also tell that they appreciated my candidness. Being that transparent with my kids was hard, but it was also like a weight was lifted off me.

"Mom, I understand how you were feeling. I felt that way too." Landon said.

"Yeah, I get that too, mom. It's hard to show someone forgiveness that doesn't deserve it." Lucy agreed.

"Mom, I get it too. I'd be lying if I said that I had felt this grace towards Fred since the beginning of all this. I was mad at first, too. I mean, I'm never going to shoot hoops with Blake again. I'm never going to get that opportunity to be his best man at his wedding. It sucks. I miss my best friend. But I know without a doubt where he is. I will always remember that peaceful smile he gave me when we were with Jesus."

All of us were in awe of Aaron's wisdom and how he was speaking so raw from his heart. We all continued to talk to one another about how we would handle everything. Nick and I told the kids not to talk about the trial at school. They all agreed.

After dropping the kids off at school, I went to talk to the attorney, that agreed to help us with this case. We talked about what to expect in the trial. First, they would be going through pictures and video footage of the accident. Then, they would probably call Aaron to the stand and possibly some of the first responders on the scene...which would include Nick.

Our attorney Janet Keating explained that she thought that Fred would be charged on two, possibly three counts. The first count would be Manslaughter in the first degree. The second count would be Manslaughter in the first degree. The third count would be transporting open bottles of alcohol because he had two open bottles of beer and one giant bottle of tequila.

When Janet told me this, I couldn't believe it. Why would Fred think it's okay to get into his truck and drive when he's drunk as a skunk? Why would he do this to other people on the road? I just didn't get it.

"So, if Fred pleads guilty, how many years would he be getting in jail then?"

"Well, Charlotte, that's where it can get tricky. First, it's up to Fred what he is going to plead...guilty or not guilty...Secondly, it's up to the legal system to decide. Then, also, that comes with the jury too. But he can get up to a life sentence. Or several years and be on probation the rest of his life."

I just sat there, taking in what Janet was saying. As crazy as it sounds, I found compassion for Fred. His dumb decision not only destroyed the lives of two families and everyone that knew and loved them, but it has destroyed his life too. I know he never really recovered after losing John Michael. He had so much anger that had controlled him for so long. Instead of turning to the Lord for healing, he turned to alcohol to numb the pain. So now he must live with the fact that he killed two people. This was the first time I thought about how Fred must be feeling.

After I left the meeting with Janet, I called Nick

and told him what had happened. Of course, he figured this was going to be the outcome. He has seen a similar situation to this one before. The drunk driver killed one person. The outcome was that the person was sentenced to eight years in prison and on probabtion for the rest of their life. I was shocked that's all they got for taking someone's life. Granted, that person probably didn't wake up that morning wanting to kill someone, but their negligence changed lives...not for the better...but for the worst. It truly is amazing how one decision can lead to life or death. One decision can reshape your future. One decision can totally transform your life.

I wonder if Fred Duncan knows the Lord...

I wonder if he relizes that he doesn't have to be enslaved to this addiction that he has to alcohol...

I found myself praying for the very man that I proclaimed to have hate for. I prayed and asked God-to soften his heart and transform his life through this situation.

I prayed that God would help him see what his negligence did to other people's lives through the trial.

I prayed that God would comfort him.

That evening, we all discussed what was said with our attorney as a family. All the kids were processing what was happening in their own way. I could tell that they all had their own unique thoughts about the possible outcomes.

But we weren't at all prepared for what was about to happen...

LIKE THIS BOOK? CHECK OUT CARRI'S OTHER BOOKS TOO!

GOD USES THE UNUSABLE

UNFAMILIAR HEROES: AUTISM "THE UNKEPT SECRET"

ENJOY THE JOURNEY

LETTING GO OF WHAT I CAN'T CONTROL

FOUNDATION STRONG

IN THIS TOGETHER

SILENCED IN JESUS NAME

GOD IS NEVER LATE

OUR PLANS < GOD'S PLANS: SHIFTING OUR PERSPECTIVE AND EXPECTATIONS

GOD MET ME THERE

Follow Carri on social!

Or visit Carri's website at
www.carrioller.com

www.ingramcontent.com/pod-product-compliance
Lightning Source LLC
Chambersburg PA
CBHW050859180626
46814CB00007B/2798